MW01144260

Trails in the Wilderness

Book 2 of the Summer Trails Series

Janessa Suderman

Scripture references are taken from the New International Version of the Holy Bible.

Cover and interior art and design by Jonathan Suderman.

ISBN: 1542490936
ISBN-13: 978-1542490931

ACKNOWLEDGMENTS

Thank you to my editors and beta-readers, especially
Jonathan Suderman, Ruth Zimmerman, Connie Sheppard,
and Amber Sokowin, for your great ideas and suggestions.
It's been a joy to share this project with you!

To keep in touch and learn about up-coming books, I
warmly welcome you to visit www.janessa.ca.

CONTENTS

Dedication i

1 Get Ready, Get Set, No! 1

2 First Night Back 8

3 Chapel Prep 18

4 Meet Virginia 27

5 Tuesday 33

6 Teepee Camp 47

7 Make Your List 63

8 A Scream in the Night 70

9 Havoc Wreaking 77

10 Blissful Oblivion 82

11 Making Things Right 86

12 Searching 91

13 Let Go 98

DEDICATION

To Davy, my little pride and joy,
and to Danny, the unsung hero who taught me to ride;
This is your tribute.

CHAPTER 1
GET READY, GET SET, NO!

"Mom!" Sixteen-year-old Jessa Davies popped her head out of her bedroom door. "Have you seen my cowboy boots? We need to go right now!" Her mother called a reply from the kitchen, but Jessa couldn't hear what she said.

Jessa gave an exasperated huff and turned her gaze back into her bedroom. The bed was heaped with a mountain of clean laundry that she hadn't gotten around to folding. Her green duffel bag was already stuffed with clothes and toiletries; she had barely been able to get the zipper closed. Now, looking at the clock, she saw that she needed to be back at camp for her wrangler staff-meeting in less than an hour.

"Mom!" Jessa screeched again.

"Jessa," Came her father's voice from down the hall, "Stop shouting. If you want to talk to your mother then go find her and talk reasonably." Jessa couldn't see her dad where he sat in his home-office, but she knew that tone and it wasn't to be questioned. Sighing, she stomped out of her room and found her mother in the kitchen. Nancy

Davies stood at the counter, mixing raw ground-beef and forming it into hamburger patties.

"I need to find my-" Jessa started, then stopped when Nancy indicated she was on the phone. Jessa hadn't noticed it tucked in the crook of her mother's neck. Jessa shoved her long, brown hair out of her face and pointed at the clock.

"And how is Alvina doing these days? Did she get into the program, then?" Nancy was saying as she placed the raw patties into a pan. Jessa motioned for her mother to hang up. Ever the social-butterfly, Nancy gave her an oblivious smile and kept chatting.

"Grr!" Jessa stalked into the mudroom and scanned the shelves but didn't see her boots there. She peeked out to the yard of the acreage. The family dog Aurelia bounded over, her tail wagging. Jessa roughed up Aurelia's fur.

"You didn't eat my boots, did you girl?" Jessa asked, a little concerned. "It wouldn't be the first time. I thought you outgrew that." Aurelia answered with a blissful 'woof' and Jessa went back inside. Clark was in the kitchen pouring himself a huge glass of chocolate milk.

"Hey, sis, don't you need to be leaving about now?" Clark asked, taunting. Jessa gritted her teeth, knowing that her older brother was just trying to get under her skin, as usual. He knew perfectly well she should have been out the door ten minutes ago. Just then she noticed something silver glinting in Clark's ear. Squinting, she stepped closer.

"Did you pierce your ear?" Jessa asked, incredulous. Clark looked pleased with himself.

"Yep. There was this wild party last night down at the park. A couple of the girls dared me to do it."

"It looks infected." Jessa said shortly. "Did you even clean the area first?"

"Nope." Clark swigged his chocolate milk. "Just rammed a safety pin through and there you have it. The girls loved it. My buddy did pour some beer on it afterwards, though. That counts, right?" Jessa looked up sharply at their mother, but it seemed she hadn't heard. Nancy was laughing into the phone and covering the pan with foil.

Clark was seventeen, and going into his senior year at the Christian school they attended. He and Jessa had always had a love-hate relationship; partly because Clark seemed to push the envelope, whereas Jessa was the stereotypical good-girl. Lately Clark had gotten 'in' with the party-crowd, and spent his evenings out with them. Jessa didn't want to know the sordid details. She just hoped he would outgrow this stage, ASAP. She saw no appeal to that lifestyle whatsoever.

"You know they'll make you take that out when we go back to school." Jessa reminded him. "The guidebook says that-"

"Yes, yes I know." Clark waved her concern away. "See, this is one of the downsides of going to a Christian school. It's full of goody-two-shoes like you."

"I'm not a goody-two-shoes!" Jessa protested, though it was a fairly accurate label. She was a straight A student, sang on the church worship team, and was spending her summer volunteering at Spruce Ridge camp, coming home only on the weekends.

"But school doesn't start up for another month. So there." Clark said, flipping his too-long wavy hair out of his eyes. "Now Jessa. You gotta hook me up with some of the hot babes at your camp."

"No way!" Jessa said.

"Come on." Clark whined. "At least introduce me. I can handle the hooking up myself."

"They wouldn't go for a guy like you. They're Christians." Jessa flung at him.

"I'm a Christian, too." He said innocently.

"Hardly." Jessa countered.

"I still believe the same things you do." Clark insisted. "I just don't see the harm in having a little fun. Playing the field, you know?"

"Forget it, Clark!" Jessa looked under the table on the off chance her boots might be there. Just then she heard a clomp-clomp-clomp shuffling into the room. She looked up and saw her little brother, Kenny, scuffling into the room, wearing only his underwear and her cowboy boots. They were far too big for his ten-year-old feet and came up to his knees.

"Hey!" Jessa laughed in spite of herself. "What do you think you're doing? I need those right now!" She reached for Kenny, but he squealed and jumped out of the way.

"But these are my new tap-shoes!" Kenny started jigging on the spot, clattering the heels all over the kitchen floor and giggling uncontrollably.

"Give them to me, you goober!" Jessa lunged at Kenny and succeeded in pinning him to the floor, pulling the boots off of him.

"Shh!" Nancy gave them a warning look and continued her conversation. Kenny was now trying on Jessa's cowboy hat, and saying in a high-pitched voice, "Hi! I'm Jessa. I think I'm so cool."

"That is mine you little pip-squeak!" Jessa swiped it off Kenny's head and crammed it over her own. She glanced in the full-length mirror near the front door. Her brown suede cowboy hat was almost the same color as her long hair. Her favourite plaid shirt and dark jeans set off her summer tan nicely.

"Time to hang out in my new bedroom!" Kenny chortled and took off towards Jessa's room.

"Mom, we have to go!" Jessa wailed, running after him.

It was a full ten minutes later that Jessa was finally out the door, lugging her duffel bag with her. Her family crowded around the door to say goodbye as Nancy started the truck. Kenny was now wearing her bathrobe and a pair of sunglasses he had swiped off her desk, and was dancing around the kitchen in them.

"See ya, dweeb." Clark teased. "Tell all your friends about what a hot-guy I am."

"Have a good week, hun." Her dad Eugene leaned forward and gave her a hug. "Call if you need anything."

"Okay, bye," Jessa hopped into the truck's passenger seat and slammed the door shut.

As soon as Nancy dropped Jessa off at the camp parking lot, Jessa said goodbye and raced to her lodge room. She flung her duffel onto her bunk and glanced at Tiff's digital alarm clock. She had three minutes to spare.

"I'm gonna be late!" Jessa bemoaned and flew down the lodge stairs and out the door. She jogged along the mulch trail that led through the camp to the barns.

Near the chapel she waved as she passed Russ, the gangly bass-player from the worship team. He was walking hand-in hand with his new girlfriend, Cory-Lynn. When camp had first started a month ago, Jessa thought maybe Russ had a crush on her. But when he realized she was only sixteen, whereas he was a bible-college student, he had quickly transferred his affections to plain, pleasant Cory-Lynn, one of the kitchen-staff. The two had just announced last week that they were going together; the first official couple of the summer.

Jessa kept jogging, passing the archery range and the climbing wall. She smiled, recalling how surprised she had been when Russ had been the first staff member to land himself a girlfriend. Russ was a nice enough person, of course. But with his over-active Adam's apple and bony limbs, he wasn't the most attractive guy on staff. Not by Jessa's standards, anyway. Then again, not many guys were as good looking as Wade.

Tall, handsome Wade, another wrangler, had come close to asking her out a few weeks ago. The spark between them had been instant and mutual. However, after a nightmarish-love triangle with Tiff, another barn-girl, Jessa had suggested they just remain friends. Yet, his blue eyes and charming smile still made her heart flutter.

At times she had to remind herself why it had seemed like a good idea to put the brakes on their budding romance.

Jessa picked up the pace as the barn came into view, ignoring the stitch in her side. She was panting by the time she reached the gate, and stopped to scrabble with the latch. Creaking it open, she strode past the stalls to the porch, where she found the barn staff lounging on the wooden benches. It was clear that the meeting had already started.

Hank, the head wrangler, paused mid-sentence and looked up at her. His bushy white eyebrows raised a little.

"Sorry I'm late." Jessa gasped, leaning against the edge of the railing to catch her breath. She nodded her greeting to her friends. Marsha, Emily and Tiff were all crammed together on one bench, and Wade and Nate sprawled wide-legged on the other. Wade looked as handsome as ever. Today he wore his leather chaps and a fringed vest. Jessa started towards him.

"Just a minute, Jessa." Hank said. "Don't sit down yet."

"What?"

"We need to speak in private." He opened the barn door and motioned towards the office. "Now." Perplexed, Jessa walked through the door.

"I'm sorry I'm late for the meeting." Jessa restated the instant Hank closed the door behind them. "Things were really crazy, and-" Hank held up a calloused hand to stop her.

"That's okay, Jessa That isn't why I asked to speak with you." Hank said.

"Oh. Okay then." Jessa instantly relaxed and settled down on the bench. It was hard and lumpy, despite being covered in horse blankets. "What's up?" Hank massaged his temples, then stroked his fuzzy white beard. Jessa thought she saw a few stray crumbs tumble out of it.

"Well, Jessa, I'm afraid we have a bit of a problem." Hank said.

"What?" Jessa asked.

"Well, do you remember last week, I mentioned that we have our special out-trips horse camp going on this week? Teepee Camp?" Hank asked.

"Vaguely." Jessa hadn't really been paying attention because she had been goofing off with Wade during that meeting. He had been tickling her knee, then looking innocent whenever Hank looked at them. "Can you remind me what that's all about, again?"

"It's a three-night special program." Hank replied. "There are six campers and two staff. They'll arrive partway through the week, and ride out past the south pastures. There's a teepee camp out there. Then they do trail rides every day, swimming in the creek, campfires, that kind of thing."

"Right." Jessa nodded. "So what's the problem?"

"I had two gals lined up to lead it. They're sisters; Stacy and Brandy, and they were wranglers here two years ago. They agreed to lead Teepee Camp for us this summer. This afternoon they called to cancel. I guess they have some family emergency." Hank told her. "So that puts us in a bit of a bind."

"I see." Jessa said, not sure what this had to do with her. Hank turned to look at her, a hopeful expression in his eyes.

"I want you to go." Hank said. "I want you to lead Teepee Camp."

CHAPTER 2
FIRST NIGHT BACK

Jessa sat numbly on the bench as Hank continued. He was already explaining that he had asked Marsha to go too.

"Since Marhsa is the more experienced wrangler, she can manage the horsemanship-side of things." Hank said. "Marsha went on Teepee Camp last summer so she knows those trails well. I was thinking you could head-up the worship and devotional times. You play guitar, right?" Jessa nodded numbly. "And you can tag-team with everything else, like the meal-prep. Tony will send down coolers of food and a cook stove-"

Jessa barely heard what Hank was saying. This was all so unexpected. She had volunteered at camp, with the intention of leading trail rides, hanging out with her friends, and eating deliciously prepared meals at the lodge. She hadn't come to babysit a bunch of campers in the wilderness for three days.

"But I can't do it." Jessa suddenly blurted out, relieved. "I didn't take the counsellor training." Hank shook his head.

"I've already cleared it with Ms. Sheila." Hank said,

referring to the camp director. "She said we could make an exception in these circumstances."

"But what about all the work here at the barn?" Jessa said. "With Marsha and I gone, the workload would be too heavy for the others to manage."

"I called in a favour from my niece, Virginia. She'll be arriving first thing in the morning, and she will help out at the barn." Hank said. Jessa conjured up an image of a female-version of Hank: solid, stocky, and tanned, though of course she wouldn't have the big white beard. The mental picture made her want to burst out laughing.

"So? Are you willing to do it?" Hank asked. Jessa paused. He was asking her to give up a week at the barn; a week with all her friends, and Wade, and the comforts of her lodge-room. She wouldn't get to work with Fairlight, her sweet little project-horse. Yet, she knew Hank was expecting her to say yes.

"Okay." She finally said. "I'll do it."

"Wonderful." Hank's furrowed brow relaxed and he clapped her on the shoulder. "I knew you'd be a good sport, Jessa. You might even have some fun with it."

"Uh-huh." Jessa shrugged.

"Alrighty, let's get back to the meeting." Hank led her back to the porch, where the others were chatting. "She said yes!" Hank announced.

"Whoo-hoo!" Marsha cheered, beaming at her. "This is awesome! We're going to have so much fun, Jessa!" Jessa sat down beside Wade, who had moved over to make room for her.

"Hey." She said, giving him a tiny wink.

"Howdy." He answered, tipping his hat to her.

"Let's get back to it, gang." Hank said. "We've got a bunch of info to cover for this week." Jessa half-listened. She was thinking about Teepee Camp. She could see the horse-herd in their paddock from where she sat, and noticed Dusty nipping at Blondie. Dusty was her favourite horse at camp; a gentle brown horse with a distinctive shaggy mane. He was the horse she had learned on, and more importantly, he was the reason she loved riding. He was still her top go-to, if she had a choice. Jessa hoped Hank would let her take him to Teepee Camp.

Before long the dinner bell was ringing through the trees, and they were free to walk back to the lodge. Marsha fell into step beside Jessa.

"So why were you so late?" Marsha ran her hand through her cropped curls. It had taken Jessa a while to get used to Marsha's unusual looks; she was over six feet tall and extremely slender, with chocolate-brown skin, bleached-blonde hair, and neon-coloured nail polish. She was also one of the friendliest people Jessa had ever met.

"Ugh." Jessa groaned, walking quickly to keep up with Marsha's long stride. Tiff hoofed-it along on Marsha's other side. "My crazy brothers happened, that's what. Kenny was dancing around like a maniac in my cowboy boots, and Clark was being a jerk, trying to get me to hook him up with a girl from camp. Plus my mom was on the phone"-

"Hold on!" Tiff stopped Jessa's tirade, a mischievous glint in her eye. "Is this the Clark we saw a picture of last week? The cute one?"

"I guess he's cute in an annoying way"-

"Maybe you should set one of us up with him." Marsha elbowed Jessa playfully, knocking her off course.

"Hey! Ow." Jessa rubbed her ribs. "He's not your type."

"Why?" Marsha quizzed. "Too short?"

"Probably." Jessa answered. "Plus he's a bit of a wild card these days. Womanizer. Heart breaker. You know? He's my brother and I love him, but he's bad news on the dating front. He's already dated two of my friends from youth-group."

"Speaking of dating." Marsha lowered her voice, glancing sideways at Tiff. "Are you going to tell her about...?"

"Not here!" Tiff whispered hoarsely. "Too many people. I'll tell you later, Jessa." Tiff was a stern-looking girl with long black braids. She and Jessa hadn't gotten along well at first; when they had both had a crush on Wade. But they had called a truce and gotten along fine since then.

"If it's about Russ and Cory-Lynn, I already know they're dating. I was there last week when they announced it." Jessa offered.

"It's not about them." Tiff said confidentially. "I'll tell you after dinner."

When the wranglers arrived at the lodge, dinner was in full swing. Most of the staff had already filled their plates and were seated randomly at the round-tables in the dining hall. Tomorrow a new batch of campers would arrive and the noise level in here would triple. Jessa went through the line, ready to load her tray with casserole and salad. She wondered if her family was just now sitting down to dinner, too, and biting into the fresh hamburgers Nancy had made.

"One scoop or two?" Tony asked her from behind the counter, ready to dish her up. It was difficult to distinguish what sort of casserole it was; there was a hodgepodge of colors in the pan. However, Tony's cooking had never disappointed her yet.

"Two please." Jessa held up her plate.

"Hank says you and Marsha are doing Teepee Camp this week." Tony said. "Come talk to me when you can and we'll go over the menu. I'll have one of the support staff bring down the big cooler and all the cookware in the truck."

"Salad?" Cory-Lynn stood ready over a huge salad bowl with tongs raised. She wore a beige apron splattered in stains, and her round cheeks were pink.

"Thanks." Jessa grabbed a fork and headed straight for the wrangler-table, where Nate was smothering his casserole with ketchup.

"Do you want some casserole with that?" Marsha mocked him as she pulled up a chair.

"Hey. C'mon. I like ketchup on my ketchup." Nate mumbled, his mouth full.

"Gross." Marsha dug in to her meal as the rest of the wranglers arrived.

"So." Wade said, looking across the table at Jessa and Marsha. "You two get to go camping in the teepees this week."

"You bet." Marsha answered, spearing a cherry tomato with her fork and popping it in her mouth.

"I'm jealous." Wade looked at Jessa with a roguish smile. Their eyes locked for a moment, then Jessa tore her gaze back to her plate. It was moments like this that she wished she hadn't suggested a 'let's just be friends' pact. He was just so, well, the best word she could think of to describe him was *hot*. She hoped there might be another chance for something more between them down the road, once camp was over.

The meal was pleasant and merry, with plenty of good conversation and laughter. Afterwards all the staff wandered over to the chapel. All the wranglers sat together in one pew near the back. Jessa was beside Tiff.

"Hey," She leaned closer to Tiff. "Can you tell me the secret now?" Tiff opened her mouth to speak, but didn't get the words out. Jay, the worship leader, had stepped up to the microphone.

"Welcome back, staffers!" He hollered, "How was everybody's weekend off?" The crowd cheered, and Jay cued the worship band to start the music. For the next half-hour the chapel was filled with worship. Jessa closed her eyes and sang with all her might. The last song was one of her favourites.

Jesus, You are the Prince of Peace
Jesus, You are the Lord of my Life
Jesus, You are the King of my heart
Everything I am is yours

I lay my life in your hands, Lord
Lead me by still waters again
Let me lie down in green pastures
You restore my soul, Jesus
I'll never let you go, Jesus.
You are the prince of Peace.

After the worship time, Russ stepped up to the microphone and selected someone from the audience to come read a bible verse. Not surprisingly he chose Cory-Lynn. Blushing, she made her way to the front and read Proverbs 4:20-23.

"My son, pay attention to what I say; turn your ear to my words. Do not let them out of your sight, keep them within your heart; for they are life to those who find them and health to one's whole body. Above all else, guard your heart, for everything you do flows from it."

"Let's hear it for the stunningly beautiful, Cory-Lynn!" Russ squeaked into his microphone. He introduced the chapel speaker, Bill, then joined Cory-Lynn and draped his arm around her. They were seated several rows in front of Jessa. Bill spoke for the next twenty minutes about 'guarding your heart', but Jessa had a hard time paying attention. She kept zoning out and watching Russ stroking Cory-Lynn's back, or playing with her hair, or whispering in her ear, until Jessa felt like screaming into a pillow. *At least they'll have to cool it when the campers are here, thank God, according to the rule-book*, Jessa thought.

After chapel, Jessa was heading for the door when she heard someone calling her name. Turning, she saw Jay striding towards her through the crowd. Today a beanie-style hat held his long yellow dread-locks back, and as usual he wore a very bright, clashing outfit.

"Hey, Jessa. How's it going?" He motioned for her to follow him to the side of the room, where it was quieter.

"It's good." She said, seeing Wade and Nate leaving chapel out of the corner of her eye.

"We need to have a conversation." Jay said pleasantly.

"Would tomorrow work for you? How about nine am, right after breakfast, here in the chapel?"

"Okay." Jessa agreed. "What about?"

"Ms. Sheila told me you would be leading worship down at Teepee Camp this week." Jay said. "I need to go over some worship music with you and make sure you have everything you need."

"Oh, okay great." Jessa said. "Would you happen to know if there's a spare guitar around I can borrow, too?"

"You play?" Jay brightened.

"A little." Jessa shrugged. "Not like you can, of course." She felt awkward the moment she said it. He was a good musician, but she didn't want him to think she was buttering him up, like some adoring groupie might.

"That's great. Sure, I have an extra acoustic in my mini-van. I'll scrounge it up for you and bring it tomorrow." Jay said. "See you here at nine."

Jessa tagged along with a few of the counsellors on their walk back to the lodge. Evening snack was cookies, and most of the staff were milling around the kitchen, talking as they ate. Jessa grabbed two big cookies and a milk to-go, then took the stairs two at a time, stuffing cookies into her mouth as she went. They were still warm, and deliciously chocolatey and crumbly. Jessa took a cool swig of milk and used her shoulder to shove open her lodge room door.

Marsha and Tiff were sprawled out on the floor, while Emily was curled up on her bed with a book. Jessa crammed the last bite of cookie in her mouth, half-tempted to run downstairs and get two more.

"So." She said, cookie-crumbs spraying out of her mouth and dropping to the floor. "Whoops, sorry. What's the deal? What's the big secret?"

Tiff sat up straight. "Okay. But you have to keep this quiet." She said, fixing her dark eyes on Jessa. Jessa nodded and gulped some milk, then glanced at Emily's bed questioningly. "It's okay, she already knows." Tiff told her, then stood and walked to the dresser. She rummaged in one of the drawers and produced a crumpled envelope.

"Here." Tiff said robotically. "Read it." Jessa took the envelope, smudging it with her chocolatey fingers. Tiff was already pacing, an anxious frown etched across her brows. Jessa opened a hand-written letter and began to read.

My darling Tiff,

I miss you so much. The time we have spent apart has been unbearable. I must be with you again, no matter what it takes, because I know you are the only one for me. We are destined for each other. I know when we broke up it seemed like the right decision at the time; but now I regret letting you go.

I didn't come back to camp this year because I wanted to try other things. To be honest, I've fallen away from the Lord. I don't know what to believe anymore, or even if God is real. I feel like a lost soul but I don't know how to get back to God. I don't even know if I want to.

But I do believe in us, Tiff. I want to get back together with you. If you will take me back; I'll come back to camp for the rest of the summer. Maybe you will be the one who can lead me back to God. I just need you to say yes.

Let me know.

Yours Truly,

Brady.

Jessa looked up at Tiff, incredulous. "Whoa." She said. "This guy is really nuts about you, isn't he?"

"What the heck am I supposed to do?" Tiff cried, clearly unable to hold it in any longer. "Does he think I'll just go running back to him?"

"Wait, wait, back up." Jessa said, sitting down on the edge of her bed. "I've never met this Brady guy. I don't even know anything about him except that you guys dated last summer."

"Allow me." Marsha jumped in. "Brady was here last summer, on the maintenance crew. He pursued Tiff for weeks before she finally went out with him, then they went steady all summer. He seemed like a strong Christian guy.

Always talking about 'the Lord' this and 'the Lord' that. But then after the summer they drifted apart because they go to different schools-"

"And plus I realized we had nothing in common." Tiff put in. "So I called him in the winter and officially ended it. I haven't heard from him since."

"So now he wants to get you back?" Jessa scanned the letter again. "And he's saying he's not a Christian anymore."

"Exactly!" Tiff threw herself down on her bunk and clapped a hand over her eyes.

"Well, do you want to get back together with him or not?" Jessa asked cautiously. She hoped Tiff would say no. She wasn't sure why but she didn't like the sound of this guy.

"I don't know." Tiff said miserably. "It wasn't all bad, dating him. He was a good boyfriend, I guess. I feel guilty saying no. He needs to get the Lord back in his life. I know if I agree to take him back, he'll be here at camp, where he has the best chance of coming back to Jesus. Maybe it's my duty to say yes, so he can get his heart right with God."

"No!" Marsha expounded. "His walk with the Lord is his responsibility, not yours."

"I agree." Jessa said. "Even though I've never had a boyfriend. Emily, what do you think?" Emily pulled herself out of her book and peered over the edge of her bunk.

"I don't know. Maybe it could be a good thing. Aren't we supposed to encourage each other in our walk with God? Build each other up? Maybe God wants to use Tiff to help Brady come back to the Lord."

"Ugh." Tiff punched her pillow viciously. "I can't deal with this right now. He's just going to have to wait for his answer until I can think this through properly."

"The thing is-" Marsha ventured timidly, "I thought you had a crush on Wade?"

"Not anymore." Tiff huffed. "I thought maybe I did

at the beginning of summer, but he's made it perfectly clear that he sees me as a buddy, or like a sister. I'm okay with that now. In fact I was looking forward to having a little less drama for the second half of the summer. I guess that was wishful thinking."

CHAPTER 3
CHAPEL PREP

The next morning after breakfast, Jessa split off from her friends and walked to the chapel alone. It felt strange knowing that the others would be going on to the barn without her; herding in the horses, saddling the trail-string, and leading trail rides. Even Marsha went with them to start preparing for Teepee Camp. Hank had relieved them of all regular barn-duties for the week, as their top priority was prepping for Teepee Camp.

Jessa had brushed her hair into a high ponytail, and wore jeans, cowboy boots, and a t-shirt. She had skipped the make-up as usual, but felt fresh and pretty to start the new day. On the short walk to the chapel she breathed in the piercing scent of spruce needles. The morning sun was slicing through the trees, alighting the forest floor. Several birds were whistling their songs back and forth. *I love the country!* Jessa thought to herself. She knew she was blessed to have grown up on an acreage. Most of her co-workers lived in the big city, and summers at this country retreat were a rare novelty.

The chapel was a long, low-building with beige stucco

walls. The asphalt shingles were curling up and probably should have been replaced years ago. Jessa pushed open the swinging door and breathed in the slightly musty, but comforting smell of the old building. It was empty now except for Jay. He was crouched in the front pew, strumming quietly on a guitar and tuning the strings as he went.

Jessa walked up the aisle towards the front, noticing that Jay wore his usual morning apparel of flannel pyjama pants and a hooded sweater pulled up over his yellow dread-locks. Generally he didn't put daywear on until lunchtime; and then he would put on the wildest, brightest shirts Jessa had seen anywhere. She wondered if he dressed that way at Bible College, too, where he was studying to become a worship pastor. Or maybe it was just his camp-look.

"You made it." Jay stood up. "I think I've got this bad-boy just about tuned up for you." He held up the guitar and a pick. "It's been stuffed under the back-seat of my minivan since I drove out from bible school, but it should work just fine for your camp-out."

"Thanks." Jessa took it and looped the strap over her head.

"Do you have any ideas for what songs you might want to do ?" Jay asked, pulling out an over-full binder. "If you want we can make some photocopies to send down with you." Over the next twenty minutes, they went through the binder and selected several camp worship songs that Jessa felt she would be able to play.

"Some of these are more fun, jumping-around camp songs." Jay said. "Those are great for getting the kids engaged. But let's also try to choose worship songs that focus more on the Lord."

"What do you mean? Don't they all?" Jessa looked through the lyrics of one of the popular worship songs she knew well.

"Well, some of these songs are telling a story, or

quoting a bible verse." Jay said. "Others are all about 'me' and how I'm doing. The true heart of worship, though, is taking the focus off of us, and putting it on the Lord." Jay said. "It's not being so fixated on analysing what we are going through. That's secondary. No matter what we're feeling, we can praise God and just thank him for who he is, without asking him for anything. You know?" He flipped a few pages and found another lyrics sheet. "See how this one is purely a praise song; there's no mention of me and how I'm dealing with life?"

"I thought we were supposed to bring our worries and stuff to God." Jessa argued.

"Of course. The bible says we are supposed to 'Bring everything with prayer and petition, giving thanks to God.' Jay quoted scripture. "I don't remember exactly where in the bible that's from, but it's in there. Sometimes we get so focused on ourselves and our needs, we forget to just worship God for who he is and what he's done for us." Jay explained. "There's something freeing about getting the focus off ourselves and just worshipping God, no matter what chaos is going on in our own lives."

Jessa nodded, understanding better what he meant. "So how do I choose what songs to do?"

"You need to pray about it." Jay stated simply. "Ask God to help show you which songs the campers need to hear. Then do your preparations, but let go of the control and let God do what he wants to do throughout the worship time." Jessa didn't quite know what Jay meant but she nodded. She had often sung on her church worship team, but she hadn't been responsible for leading it before.

"Let's try playing a couple of these," Jay picked up another guitar and tuned it. "I'll play along with you." The two played through a few songs together, with Jay giving her some feedback about pacing and strumming.

"You know, you really have a pretty voice." He commented after a few songs. "It's a shame it hasn't worked out for you to join the camp worship team."

"It's just too crazy at the barn." Jessa apologized.

Just then, the chapel door opened and Russ and Cory-Lynn strolled in, holding hands and looking like they were on cloud nine.

"Hey dudes." Russ said as he loafed over. Cory-Lynn was beaming and wrapped her arms around Russ's skinny waist.

"Hey, bro!" Jay stood up and gave Russ a high-five. "Where'd you guys head off to this morning? I didn't see you at breakfast."

"Tony gave me the morning off." Cory-Lynn said, "So we took a picnic breakfast down to the creek."

"We thought we better get a date in before the campers arrive today." Russ explained. "Hey, Jay, I needed to confirm with you about that one song for tonight-" The guys drifted towards the sound-booth and Cory-Lynn sat down beside Jessa. Jessa started gathering up papers and putting them in order.

"Well, it sure seems like you two are getting closer than ever!" Jessa said congenially. She didn't know Cory-Lynn too well but had always found her quite pleasant.

"Oh, yes Russ is just fantastic." Cory-Lynn agreed enthusiastically. "Can you believe it? He said about a week ago, when I was serving him a cinnamon roll during snack-time, it suddenly hit him like a thunderclap that I was the only girl for him. Isn't that amazing?"

"Wow." Jessa said flatly.

"I know!" Cory-Lynn exclaimed. "And then, just now down at the creek, he did the most romantic thing in the whole world."

"What?" Jessa asked as Cory-Lynn leaned in closer.

"He washed my feet!"

"Washed your feet?" Jessa repeated, confused. "Why, were they dirty?" Cory-Lynn giggled.

"No, silly. It's a symbolic gesture. Don't you remember in the bible, that Jesus himself washed the disciples feet? And then Jesus told the disciples they should wash each other's' feet." Jessa had heard those bible verses before but didn't see what it had to do with Russ and Cory-Lynn.

"Don't you see?" Cory-Lynn said, noticing the blank look on Jessa's face. "It's an act of love and devotion. It's a way to serve someone else. To lower yourself to wash someone else's feet is a symbol of servanthood and love. Russ loves me!"

"Oh!" Jessa said. "Okay, I get it now." She nodded encouragingly. "But, are you sure it really means he loves you? I mean you only started dating a week ago."

"Oh I know he loves me." Cory-Lynn said confidently, brushing her bangs off her moist brow.

"How do you know?"

"Because he already told me."

Jessa hoped she would have a chance to get down to the barn later that morning, but it didn't happen. As soon as she was done prepping the worship music, the chapel speaker Bill walked in and said that it was an ideal time to talk about leading campfire devotions. By the time that was over, it was already lunchtime.

Jessa walked back to the lodge with Jay, bringing along his spare guitar. She would keep it in her lodge-room until Wednesday, then it would be brought down to the teepees by whoever came with the food-coolers and luggage. The hot July sun was overhead now, hitting Jessa directly on top of her head.

"So, it looks like Russ and Cory-Lynn are getting pretty serious already." Jessa said to Jay casually.

"Hmm." Jay said. "I guess so."

"Seems kind of fast, doesn't it?" She asked. She didn't want to pry, but Jay was one of Russ's closest friends. They were roommates at bible college, and Jessa wondered if this fast-moving relationship was as startling to Jay as it was to her.

"I suppose when you know, you know.'" Jay answered. "Though I myself am more of a proponent of the whole 'Love is patient' thing. Like it says in first Corinthians thirteen. What's the hurry?"

"I agree." Jessa said, thinking of Wade.

"But then again," Jay qualified quickly. "Maybe I'm wrong. I mean, my own parents knew within weeks of meeting that they were going to get married, and now thirty years later they are still happy together."

"Speaking of parents," Jessa remembered, "I need to give mine a call before lunch. See you later?" She opened the lodge door and turned towards the stairs.

"Sure. Let me know if you need anything else for the worship prep." Jay waved and walked towards the kitchen. Jessa climbed the stairs and reached the staff lounge. She scooped up the staff-phone and sprawled out on the floral couch, dialling her parent's number. She listened to it ring three, four times and was just about to give up when she heard her brother's voice.

"Hello?"

"Clark?" Jessa asked.

"Yep. And this must be my annoying kid-sister." His voice came through teasing. "You must be calling to tell me when I can come meet up with your hot friends."

"You wish." Jessa answered. "I need to talk to mom and dad."

"Mom and Kenny aren't here, and dad is in his office."

"Can you get him?" Jessa said impatiently. She wanted to get down to lunch in time to eat with her friends. She had already missed the whole morning with them.

"Okay, I'll get him." Clark said. "*If* you agree to set me up with someone."

"In your dreams!" Jessa shot out.

"Tut-tut. Such a temper." Clark taunted. "I guess I

may as well hang up then. Have a good summer, kid."

"Wait!" Jessa yelped. "I'm serious, Clark, give the phone to dad."

"You'll introduce me to some of your friends?"

"Fine." Jessa agreed. She would introduce him, and then her friends would see for themselves that he was not dating-material. He would have to learn to handle the rejection. A minute later her dad was on the phone.

"How's our girl?" Her father's voice came through warmly. Jessa explained about how she had been asked to go to Teepee Camp as a counsellor. She half hoped her dad would say she couldn't do it. That way she would have the perfect excuse to tell Hank, and she would get to stay at the barn.

"Sounds fantastic. Have fun." Her dad said, causing her to slump a little. "And one of us will come pick you up this Saturday as usual."

"Okay." Jessa agreed. By the time she had hung up and gone to the dining room, lunch was nearly over. She grabbed a plate and went alone to the serving counter. She loaded a crisp quesadilla on her plate and took several melon slices, then headed into the dining room. She saw that several staff had already left, probably to prepare for the campers who would be arriving soon. Nate and Marsha were both still at the wrangler table, though, so Jessa joined them. She bit into her cool quesadilla and chewed happily.

"Hey, where have you been?" Nate asked.

"I had to get ready for Teepee Camp. Worship leading prep." Jessa said after she had swallowed. "How were things at the barn this morning?"

"Interesting." Marsha answered, giving her a strange look. "The new girl arrived. Hank's niece, Virginia."

"Oh, right." Jessa dipped her quesadilla in sour cream, not particularly interested. "And what's she like? Does she look like Hank?" To that Nate, who had just taken a drink of juice, burst out laughing. He turned beet-red and grabbed at a napkin, but it was too late. Juice squirted out of his nose and sprayed the table, his eyes watering.

"Sick!" Marsha cried, yanking extra napkins from the dispenser and tossing them at him. "Aren't boys nasty?" She said to Jessa.

"What was so funny?" Jessa asked. Nate tried to compose himself.

"It's just that, well, Virginia looks absolutely nothing like Hank." He said. "Nothing."

"Okay then?" Jessa said. When it was clear Nate wasn't going to say anything more, she let it go, figuring she would find out for herself what Virginia was like right after lunch. The three walked back to the barn together a short time later, and arrived to find Tiff and Emily cleaning out the stalls. Nate joined them, admitting that it was his turn to do 'poo-patrol' anyway.

"So," Marsha said, "Why don't we head into the paddock and take a look at the horses? I have a pretty good idea which horses I want to bring on Teepee Camp, but I want your opinion."

"Sure." Jessa agreed. "I want to say hi to Fairlight, too." She thought of the beautiful golden filly she had taken on as her project-horse. Over the past few weeks she had spent plenty of time grooming her and leading her around with a halter. Fairlight was sweet and friendly and seemed to especially like Jessa, too.

Jessa followed Marsha to the horse paddock, where the herd of forty horses milled in the afternoon sun. They were swatting at flies with their tails and relaxing with eyes half-closed. Marsha went straight to Brutus, her project horse, and started patting his neck.

"Hey cute lil buddy." She crooned, ruffling up his dark mane. "How's lil Brutus?"

"I'm going to look for Fairlight," Jessa told her, and walked on through the herd. She thought she heard a gentle mumble of voices coming from the farthest part of the paddock, but she couldn't see because Leviathan stood in her way.

"Get out of the way, Leviathan," Jessa elbowed his huge grey rump until he stepped lazily aside, then she stopped short, frozen to the spot. Up against the fence was Fairlight, and she wasn't alone. Wade stood right next to her, with his arm wrapped around the prettiest girl Jessa had ever seen.

CHAPTER 4
MEET VIRGINIA

Jessa stood rooted in place, unable to move. Wade saw her and removed his arm from the girl, waving at her casually.

"Hey, Jessa, how's it goin'? This is Virginia." He said warmly. The girl turned, and Jessa stared dumbly.

Virginia had perfectly clear skin, rosebud lips, and huge baby-doll eyes accentuated by precisely applied make-up. Her golden hair flowed down her slender back. She stood at least three inches shorter than Jessa; her petite, curvy frame clad in tight jeans and immaculate, embroidered cowboy boots.

"Such a delight." Virginia smiled demurely at Jessa, revealing straight, white teeth. "I hear I'll be taking your place this week."

"Taking my place?" Jessa repeated weakly, looking back at Wade.

"Of course." Virginia answered. "Aren't you going to Teepee Camp? That's what my Uncle Hank said."

"Oh. Yeah. Right." Jessa stammered as Virginia stroked Fairlight's tawny neck. "That's my- I mean, that's

27

Fairlight."

"I know." Virginia said, her voice velvety. "I've pretty much decided to adopt her."

"Adopt?" Jessa said, cold fingers of dread squeezing her heart.

"Well she's the prettiest horse here! I've vetted them out and decided she's something special. Don't you think?" Virginia said.

"She is lovely." Wade added, looking straight at Virginia rather than Fairlight. Panicking, Jessa stepped forward.

"Sorry but she's not available for 'adoption'. She's already taken. She's my project horse for the summer." Jessa blurted out awkwardly, just as Fairlight nuzzled Virginia's palm. Virginia laughed, her silky voice lilting through the air.

"I don't know about that, Jessa. It looks like she's decided to adopt me, too!" Virginia said sweetly.

"But-" Jessa said, her temper rising.

"Kidding!" Virginia said. Jessa forced herself to chuckle along. "How about if I keep an eye on her for you while you're gone?" Jessa told herself to calm down. Of *course* Hank wouldn't just let someone else take over with Fairlight. Would he?

"Why don't I introduce you to the rest of the herd?" Wade said to Virginia, offering his arm to her. She laughed and took his arm.

"Nice to meet you, Jessa!" Virginia said and strolled away with Wade. Fairlight followed after Virginia, nickering in protest. *Come back here you little traitor!* Jessa wanted to yell at Fairlight. *You're supposed to be MY little buddy!* Jessa could hear Virginia laughing again at something Wade had said. She glanced over to them where they were now patting Wade's horse, Bea. Wade boosted Virginia up on Bea's back, and placed his own cowboy hat on Virginia's head.

Shaking her head, Jessa turned and walked to find

Marsha. She was seething. It was one thing for Virginia to try to take Fairlight from her, but now Wade? It couldn't be clearer that he was taken with the new girl. Jessa felt suddenly self-conscious about her silly high-pony tail. She must look like a wanna-be cheerleader. She wished she had taken the time to put some make-up on that morning, after all.

Marsha was still petting Brutus near the gate. Jessa stormed over, her brows furrowed.

"Hi! Oh, hey, what's wrong?" Marsha asked.

"It's Virginia." Jessa whispered.

"What?" Marsha asked. "She seemed really sweet this morning. Everyone is quite taken with her."

"Exactly." Jessa said. "Including Fairlight. But especially Wade. Have you noticed that?"

"Is he?" Marsha frowned. "I know Nate thought she was pretty, but I don't know about Wade."

"I definitely think she's going after him." Jessa fumed. "It's disgusting. She's so flirty and obvious! Surely he can see right through that?" Marsha actually stepped back, looking alarmed.

"Look." Marsha said. "I don't know why this bothers you anyway, even if he does like her. Didn't he want to ask you out, and you said no? I thought you got over him?"

"Still." Jessa flung out. "Everyone is pairing up around here. Has everyone forgotten why we came here? This is about serving God and telling campers about Jesus. Not, not...hooking up!"

"Jessa." Marsha put her hands on Jessa's shoulders. Her brown eyes looked sternly into Jessa's. "I'm going to say this with love, and as a friend. Let. It. Go. You're totally overreacting here, and it's only going to cause drama."

Jessa shook off Marsha's bony hands from her shoulders, irritated. "Fine." She grumbled. "I probably am overreacting." Jessa reached out to pat Brutus as well, running her fingers through his reddish-brown coat.

"It's just that..." She trailed off. "Never mind. Let's pick out our horses for Teepee Camp."

"And you'll be nice to Virginia?" Marsha reminded her. "Remember she's the new girl here. And she's only here the one week, apparently."

"Yes, of course." Jessa grudgingly replied. "I'll be perfectly nice." The two girls left Brutus and walked among the herd, trying to choose the calmest horses. Jessa suggested Peaches, Jewel, and Vixen. Marsha agreed, and suggested Blondie and Elf, then craned her neck to look around some more.

"The other one that would be good would be Chester." Marsha said, squinting. "I don't see him around here. Let's keep looking. He's really old and calm, so he's the perfect camp horse for a scared, newbie rider."

"And who will you be riding?" Jessa said, remembering she needed to ask Hank if she could take Dusty. She leaned over to give Dusty an affectionate scrub on the neck as they passed him. Dusty grunted lazily in response.

"I'll probably take Jinx. I've been having fun with him lately." Marsha decided. The girls combed the herd and didn't see Chester. They did see Wade and Virginia again, still talking and laughing like they were having the time of their lives.

"Have you guys seen Chester?" Marsha interrupted them. Wade shook his head.

"I don't think so. I can't remember if I saw him during the herd-in this morning. But Hank took a couple horses to the west paddock yesterday, because the vet's coming to float their teeth tomorrow. Maybe Chester's in there." He said, as Virginia slid off Bea's back.

"That makes sense." Marsha nodded. "I'll ask him." With that she and Jessa walked back to the barn.

"See?" Jessa whispered. "She was on his horse!"

"That doesn't mean anything." Marsha dismissed. "Wade's a nice guy. He's friendly to everyone. That's just who he is."

"Not *that* friendly. Did you see she was wearing his hat? And did you see the way he was looking at her?" Jessa insisted.

"No. How was he looking at her?" Marsha said, looking impatient.

"He was looking at her like..." Jessa trailed off wistfully. *Like he used to look at me,* she thought, though she didn't voice the end of her sentence.

The afternoon was busy. Marsha and Jessa didn't have a chance to talk to Hank; they were too busy getting organized for Teepee Camp. Marsha hauled a bunch of old storage tubs out of the dusty feed-room and rooted through them for leather rain-slickers, saddlebags, and a big electric lantern. Jessa packed some brushes and hoof-picks into a sack, then tossed in an equine antiseptic spray and insect-repellent.

"So let me get this straight," Jessa said to Marsha as she heaved a bag of oats onto the office counter. "The campers arrive Wednesday afternoon. We leave their bags at the lodge and bring them here. Then, we get their helmets, put them on their horses, and ride off to the teepees."

"Right." Marsha confirmed. "It's about a two-hour ride to get there, I'd say. Far enough that it's not exactly convenient to get back here in a hurry, but we're still on camp property. Someone else will drive all the stuff down there on the back roads."

It wasn't until the dinner bell gonged through the trees that Jessa remembered they still had to ask Hank about taking Chester. She walked to the lodge with the others, hanging back behind Virginia, who was talking to Wade about rodeo.

"Rodeo?" Tiff piped in, tapping Virginia on the shoulder. "What do you know about rodeo?"

"Last year I was Miss-Teen Rodeo for McTavish County." Virginia answered, running her hand through her blond curls.

"So you must be able to ride okay, then." Tiff said shortly. Jessa hid a smile. Tiff was known for her bluntness.

"Oh, I manage." Virginia replied, batting her eyelashes at Wade. "I guess I know my way around a saddle." Jessa decided she looked like a china-doll.

"You should have seen her on Bea, Tiff." Wade boasted. "Total horse-whisperer right here."

"Peachy." Tiff quipped dryly. "I take it you'll be volunteering to lead one of the horsemanship classes, then?"

"Certainly." Virginia agreed cordially. "Anything I can do to help." Jessa sidled up to Nate, realizing she had barely seen him all day.

"Hey, did you see Chester today?" She asked, nudging him. Nate shook his head.

"I didn't really see any of the herd, though. I didn't go on the morning round-up." Nate said, his eyes fixed on Virginia's tight jeans. Jessa rolled her eyes and kept quiet the rest of the way to the lodge. She was afraid if she said anything it wouldn't be all that pretty.

CHAPTER 5
TUESDAY

That evening after chapel, Jessa skipped snack and opted instead for a shower. Not necessarily because she needed one; but because she wanted some alone-time. She walked into her lodge-room to get her towel and immediately caught her feet on something. Wobbling, she lunged at the closet door and clambered for the knob, missed, and crashed into the wall; sliding down it and landing with a thump on the floor.

Sitting up, she saw that she had tripped over a mattress on the floor. It certainly hadn't been there this morning when she left the room. She noted irritably that she had missed landing on the bed by about two inches, and hit the hard floor instead. *Just my luck today.* She grumbled inwardly and struggled to her feet, her dirty cowboy boot leaving a dusty smudge on the white-lace pillowcase.

"Shoot!" Jessa tried to brush off the mark, realizing this must be Virginia's bed. A chic black sleeping bag was spread out on it, and a massive designer suitcase stood at the far end of the mattress. Unfortunately that left little floor-space in the already crowded lodge-room.

Jessa grabbed her shampoo and a towel, and trudged down the hall to the bathroom. The hot water was a tonic to her nerves, instantly melting the stress out of her neck and shoulders. She thought back to how at dinner, Virginia had charmed everyone, fluttering her long-lashes at 'Uncle Hank' and taking demure little bites of salad. Her posture was perfect and her motions poised. The worst part was that she seemed genuinely nice; so Jessa was having a hard time finding an excuse to hate her.

Lathering her hair with shampoo, Jessa let the water stream over her head. She knew she was being ridiculous, letting the new girl intimidate her like this. So what if Virginia was pretty and sweet and nice? Jessa was those things, too. *Why am I seeing her as competition?* She thought. *Am I really so pig-headed that I can't be friends with anyone who's 'better' than me?*

Jessa knew the root of her jealousy was because of Wade. He seemed so taken with Virginia. A few weeks ago, Jessa had been so sure she didn't want to pursue a relationship with him. Now that he was paying attention to someone else, Jessa wanted to get him back. *He's supposed to be flirting with ME,* she scowled. At the same time she felt petty and was relieved no one could hear her secret thoughts.

Then, she remembered with a start that someone could indeed hear her innermost thoughts.

I'm sorry. She whispered meekly to God. *I know you still love me even when I'm acting like such an idiot. Please help me let go of these jealous, bitter feelings. Help me be welcoming and friendly to Virginia.*

Oh, and help me get through this Teepee Camp camp!

Jessa thought back to chapel that night. The room had been stuffed to the rafters with giddy eight-year-olds in camp t-shirts, jumping and yelling along to the upbeat worship songs. Jay had left his dread-locks wild and loose, and wore a hot-pink Hawaiian print shirt. Then Bill had spoken, giving his typical, first day of camp salvation-message that Jessa had heard a million times. She had zoned out, opting instead to rubber-neck Virginia, who sat between Wade and Emily at the end of the row. It was hard not to stare at her.

Jessa stepped out of the shower and dried off, pulling on a clean pair of sweats. She headed back to her room, towelling off her wet hair. All the barn-girls including Virginia were playing cards.

"Hi," Tiff said, looking up from her cards. "You missed a good snack tonight. Mini-pizzas."

"Oh well." Jessa hung her towel over the rungs of the bunk-ladder. "Sorry Virginia, I got some dirt on your pillow earlier."

"No worries at all!" Virginia waved a manicured hand. "I brought an extra pillow case."

"Do you want to join us? We're playing Bumble-Q." Tiff offered, patting the carpet beside her. Jessa hesitated a moment, then agreed. She loved Bumble-Q.

"Oh, and Jessa." Tiff leaned in to whisper. She peeked at Virginia and Emily, who were momentarily distracted by a story Marsha was telling. "Tonight we need to do barn-girl initiation again. For both Virginia and Emily, this time." Jessa remembered back to her first week, when Marsha and Tiff had smuggled her out in the dead of night and thrown her in the creek. They had nearly been caught by Ms. Sheila and Nate's dad; and had assured Hank they wouldn't break curfew again.

"We can't." Jessa shook her head. "We already told Hank it wouldn't happen again."

"It's tradition." Tiff insisted. "We have to do it."

"Then you'll have to do it without me." Jessa replied, holding her ground. She had learned that the best way to communicate with Tiff was in black-and-whites.

"Fine." Tiff huffed, throwing one of her black braids over her shoulder. "I don't know why you have to be such a goody-two-shoes about it. It's all just in fun."

"Goody-two-shoes?" Jessa laughed, letting the jab slip off her. She had learned to grow a thick skin around Tiff; who didn't seem to have a sensitivity meter whatsoever. "That's exactly what Clark called me the other day. My brother."

"Maybe Clark and I would get along." Tiff teased. "Then I wouldn't have to make up my mind about the whole Brady-fiasco. I can just tell him I'm taken."

"Don't even think about it." Jessa warned.

In the end the girls agreed to postpone the midnight dip in the creek until the weekend. Tomorrow would be a full day at the barn; starting with pre-breakfast herd in, then back-to-back trails rides for most of the day. Jessa decided as she fell asleep that she wanted to get up early with the others for round up, even though Hank had said she didn't have to. Most of the rest of Tuesday would be spent preparing for the camp-out, so she wanted to get at least a short ride in. Plus it was a chance to be with Wade, and remind him that she still existed.

Jessa startled awake at five am, an hour earlier than usual, by the sound of an unfamiliar alarm.

"Sorry!" She heard Virginia whisper and rummage in her bag. The early morning light glowed through the window. Jessa rolled over and tried to get back to sleep. Virginia slipped out of the room, and all was quiet again. Just before six Virginia returned from the bathroom, looking like a movie star. Her hair had been washed and blow-dried, her make-up artfully applied, and she wore tight jeans with rhinestones stitched all down the sides.

"Morning, sleepyheads!" Virginia cooed as Tiff's six am alarm bleeped. Tiff's solid arm shot out from under her covers and hammered her fist on the 'snooze' button. Jessa rolled out of bed and pulled on some clothes. Her hair was a mess but she didn't have time now to deal with that; so she tied it back and settled her cowboy hat on her head. The other girls followed a similar morning routine. Jessa had to admit Virginia looked wonderful compared to the rest of them. As they walked out to the barn, she forced herself to be friendly.

"You look so fresh and pretty today, Virginia." Jessa said. "I guess if you're willing to give up on that extra hour of sleep, you can really look nice, hey?"

"Absolutely, darlin'!" Virginia beamed. "You are such a sweetheart, Jessa. Thanks for sayin' that. It doesn't take much. A bit of effort goes a long way." Jessa nodded, thinking that maybe she should have gotten up early, too. She didn't want to become the barn-frump, especially if she wanted to keep Wade interested.

"I'd rather have the extra sleep." Tiff declared as they reached the barn. "We all look grubby by the end of the day anyway." Tiff's braids were so tight it hadn't mattered that she'd slept in them.

"I find if I put some effort into looking good, I feel better about myself and have a better day." Virginia said serenely. "I learned that on the teen-rodeo circuit. I was supposed to be camera-ready all day long."

Jessa saddled up Flash for the herd-in, a peppy, black horse with plenty of energy. Dusty had not been kept back overnight, as Hank hadn't known she was going along for herd-in. Wade, Hank, and Nate were already there, tacking up their horses. Jessa walked past Bea's stall, where Wade was saddling her.

"Morning, Wade." Jessa said with what she hoped was a beguiling smile as she passed. "Isn't it a beautiful morning?"

"Howdy." Wade tipped his cowboy hat with a tight smile, and continued saddling Bea. *That's it?* Jessa thought indignantly as she pulled Flash's saddle off the tree-horn in the tack-room. *No 'How's the cutest filly in the herd today?' No 'not as beautiful as you?' The nerve!* She supposed she had gotten used to special attention from Wade over the past several weeks. He usually had some sweet compliment for her, or an inside joke to crack. Now it was just 'howdy'. Fine. She would show him 'howdy!'

Jessa cinched Flash's saddle and eased the snaffle-bit into his mouth. He seemed more jittery than normal today, so she gave him an extra pat on the neck. "It's okay, boy. It's gonna be fun! We get to go herd all your buddies!"

Jessa swung up into the saddle and trotted Flash towards the gate, where Hank sat waiting on his white horse, Silver. Soon everyone else had joined them, and they trotted out across the green field. They slowed to a walk on the steep path sloping down to the creek. Virginia rode Zorro, a huge black horse. She trotted ahead of the others and stopped at the creek to let Zorro drink. Wade trotted Bea over to join her, splashing a little as he approached. Jessa heard Virginia laughing and saying something to Wade. Without thinking, Jessa kicked Flash into a lope. She had to get in there and get Wade's attention!

Her approach was faster than she intended, and as Flash skidded to a stop next to Virginia his front feet plunged into the water at just the right angle to arc a huge splash over Zorro. In an instant Virginia's hair and make-up were dripping.

"Sorry!" Jessa cried, instantly regretting her rash actions. "I'm so sorry Virginia, are you okay? I honestly didn't mean to soak you-" Wade looked at her like she was crazy.

Virginia laughed so hard she had tears in her eyes. "Don't worry about it!" She said. "It's the perfect way to wake me up!" While Virginia seemed to be a good-sport about the soaking, Wade was still staring at Jessa oddly, like he couldn't believe she had done that.

"Well, we better get going!" Jessa said, escaping. She trotted Flash on through the water and towards the horse pasture. *What is the matter with me?* Jessa thought. She spotted the herd and reigned Flash in that direction. She heard a horse loping up behind her, and turned to see Tiff on Zeke; the rest of the group still far behind.

"Why did you splash Virginia like that? Were you trying to be funny?" Tiff asked, slowing Zeke to trot beside her.

"It was an accident." Jessa said lamely, seeing Dusty grazing ahead. His brown head bobbed up to look at her.

"Maybe I'm way off here, but I get the feeling you don't exactly like Virginia." Tiff said.

"She's perfectly lovely." Jessa said through gritted teeth.

"Then what's with you?" Tiff said. "You were weird all through dinner and chapel last night, just staring at her with this annoyed look. You're coming off really snobby."

"I didn't!" Jessa scowled.

"And then just now it looked like you purposely soaked her." Tiff finished. "If you're going to pretend like there's nothing going on, well, I don't buy it."

"Fine." Jessa slowed Flash to a walk, motioning for Tiff to do the same. She breathed in deeply, the honeyed-smell of clover floating upwards as Flash's hooves crushed the grass with each step. Jessa noticed Fairlight frolicking with Brutus, taking nibbles of the dewy grass.

"Fine." Jessa repeated. "I'm jealous of Virginia."

"Why?" Tiff asked.

"Because she's prettier than me, a better rider, and she's got her claws in Wade already." Jessa spewed out irritably. She felt pathetic. Tiff stopped her horse, threw back her head, and shrieked with laughter.

"What?" Jessa frowned, glancing back to the others. They were still a hundred yards back. Nate was leaning over to say something to Virginia, a mesmerized expression on his face.

"You crack me up." Tiff giggled, lowering her voice. "Oh, how the tables have turned."

"Excuse me?" Jessa was getting annoyed.

"That's exactly how I felt about you, back when we

first met. Except for being a better rider, obviously. You came here and were the golden girl everyone liked. You were all cute and sweet, and Wade was all flirty with you. Now you know what it's like. Ironic, isn't it?"

"Sure." Jessa said through gritted teeth.

"Just don't make a fool of yourself like I did." Tiff suggested. "You know, when I went all psycho and demanded you stay away from Wade. It will just cause drama."

Jessa nodded. She had almost forgotten how jealous Tiff had been of her when they first met. She decided not to say anything more, especially about Wade. It might still be a tender subject with Tiff, since she had had a huge crush on him earlier in the summer.

"Whatever. Let's forget it." Jessa said. The rest of the wranglers arrived and formed a semi-circle around the herd. They drove them back to the creek without incident, and were just herding them up the hill when Marsha trotted up beside her.

"Hey," Marsha said, her dark skin looking tawny in the morning sun. "We never did ask Hank about Chester, did we?"

"No, we didn't." Jessa said. She spotted Hank up ahead, riding with Emily and Nate. "Let's find out." She urged Flash into a lope and soon caught up to Hank, with Marsha close behind her.

"Hey Hank." Jessa said, catching her breath.

"Morning, cowgirl." Hank said congenially. "You're doing a great job on Flash lately. You've really come a long way." The sunlight reflected off Hank's white beard, and his horse's white mane, making them shimmer like silver. "Were you wanting to take Flash on Teepee Camp?"

"I was actually hoping to take Dusty." Jessa said. "If that's okay."

"Sure." Hank agreed.

"And Hank," Marsha put in, "We were talking about which horses to take, and we need to go over it with you."

"Fine." Hank said as they approached the horse paddock. Most of the horses were safely in the pen, and Tiff and Wade chased in the last stragglers. "We can go over all that at our barn-staff meeting after breakfast."

"Just one thing." Marsha said, "We wanted to take Chester, and-"

"Yes, that's fine take Chester." Hank climbed down from Silver and latched the paddock gate. "We can go over all that later. Right now we better get down to breakfast or we'll miss it."

"Okay." Marsha shrugged. Hank waved to the other riders.

"Let's run up to the lodge for breakfast." He called out, then turned Silver and nudged him into a lope. Jessa let Flash go, and the entire group galloped all the way down the wood-chip path to the lodge.

Breakfast was a hurried affair. Jessa grabbed an egg-sausage breakfast sandwich and milk, sat down for about three minutes to scarf it, and was back on Flash running for the barn. The first trail ride was in an hour, and the trail string was yet to be saddled. Jessa wasn't obligated to work at the barn today, but she decided to anyway. The wranglers flew into action, brushing and saddling the trail horses. When the stalls were full of saddled, bridled horses tied and waiting patiently for riders, the clock read nine-fifty; only ten minutes to spare until the campers arrived.

"Come on, gang!" Hank called out from inside the barn. "Wrangler meeting in the office, now." Jessa headed in to the office. Hank had taken off his cowboy hat, revealing a ridge in his forehead and hair, indicating that his cowboy hat was a tad snug. He was also wearing a too-tight hoodie with an athletic logo on the front, which looked odd on him.

"Hey." Nate pointed at Hank's torso as he entered the office. "Is that my hoodie? I left it on the coat-hook."

"Might be." Hank shrugged, unconcerned. "Okay gang. Let's get to it. Here's the schedule on the whiteboard," He gestured behind him. "As you see we have a full day. Four trail rides before lunch, two after lunch, then horse-care and horsemanship classes." He turned to his niece.

"Virginia, I have you flanking trail-rides today, so you can get to know the area. Sound good?"

"Sounds good, Uncle Hank." Virginia answered with her winning-smile.

"Okay." Hank said, stuffing his hands into the hoodie's front pocket. He found a packet of gum and crinkled one out of the plastic pocket, popping it in his mouth. "Don't mind if I do."

"Uh, enjoy?" Nate snorted.

"Head out, gang. Except Marsha and Jessa. Let's take a minute to talk Teepee Camp." Hank said as the others filed out. "So. Gals. Tell me the ugly." Jessa and Marsha exchanged side-ways glances. Hank was always entertaining when in his goofy mood.

"Well, we want to take Peaches, Chester, Vixen, Elf, Jewel, and Blondie." Marsha listed off on her long fingers. "And Jinx and Dusty for ourselves."

"Fine." Hank agreed. "I'll make sure they're saddled and ready to go for you when you get here tomorrow with the campers. I think that's a two o clock ride-out, to get to the teepees and set-up by dinner time."

"So, we can take Chester then?" Marsha confirmed.

"Of course." Hank looked puzzled. "Why wouldn't you?"

"I just thought maybe he needed his teeth floated." Marsha shrugged. "I assumed you put him in the other pen for when the vet comes."

"He just got his teeth done in April." Hank said. "So he's good to go."

"Okay, we're all good then?" Jessa stood to leave.

"Wait a minute." Marsha said. "If he's not in the vet-pen, then where is he?"

"Should be in with the herd, I presume." Hank

42

answered.

"We didn't see him in the herd yesterday," Marsha explained. "We specifically looked for him, didn't we Jessa?" Jessa nodded

"What about this morning? Did either of you see Chester?" Hank walked to the door, motioning for them to join him. Jessa followed them into the horse paddock and again scanned the herd. After walking around the pen twice, Hank shook his head, his brow furrowed.

"He's not here. And he definitely isn't saddled for trails today." Hank peered down the outdoor corridor between the stalls.

"So, he's not in a different pen, then?" Marsha asked.

"Not that I know of." Hank stroked his beard thoughtfully. "I wonder if he got out into that oat field again. Last fall five or six of them escaped into the neighbour's place."

"Some of the mares and babies got out a few weeks ago, too." Jessa remembered. "Isn't that dangerous? If he eats too much oats and gets sick?" Hank nodded.

"Could." He said. "Tell you what. It's way too busy around here today to go looking for him. You two go ahead and finish your Teepee Camp prep, and I'll give the neighbours a call; see if he wandered over there again. If we haven't seen him by this evening a couple of us will ride out after dinner and look for him."

For the rest of the day, Jessa and Marsha got organized for the camp-out. They met with Tony and Cory-Lynn to go over the menu and cookware. Jessa also figured out which clothes she needed to bring. By dinnertime she was fairly sure she was all ready to go. Her campers would arrive tomorrow after lunch, and they would walk over to the barn and ride away from there.

Jessa and Marsha went to dinner together and were

the first ones at the barn-staff table. A heavy rainstorm had rolled in, so many of the campers had come to dinner muddy and wet. Jessa leaned back in her chair to look out the nearest window. It was fogging up. The sky was dark with clouds, but illuminated by the occasional flash of lightening. Raindrops pattered on the window and streaked down it, blurring the spruce trees that bordered the lodge. Just before she looked away, Jessa thought she saw the shapes of three horses moving past towards the hitching rails.

A few minutes later, Hank, Virginia, and Wade entered the dining hall, all wearing leather chaps and slickers. Carrying plates of food, they bustled over to join Marsha and Jessa.

"Hi, y'all." Virginia smiled. "This storm is a doozy, isn't it?"

"Hi Virginia." Jessa said politely. "Where's everyone else, Hank?"

"They're on their way down here on foot, so they should be here soon." Hank said, squirting mustard on his hamburger. "These two and I brought a couple horses down, and after a quick bite we'll ride straight out to the pasture and look around for Chester."

"In this storm?" Marsha asked incredulously. "It's so dark and rainy out, though."

"Still," Hank said, "A good shepherd takes care of all his sheep. Even if just one is lost, he goes out to find it."

"We're talking about horses here, Hank." Marsha reminded him.

"I know." Hank bit into a handful of chips. "I was referring to the bible verse that says Jesus is our shepherd, and if one of us gets lost he comes out into the night and finds us." He crunched his chips. "I actually feel bad I didn't notice Chester was missing until now. I realized I haven't seen him since last Friday. He could have been gone for days; could be miles from here by now."

"Where do you think he went?" Jessa asked. Hank

shrugged.

"Could be anywhere. He could have wandered over to a neighbour's property, or gotten in with someone else's horses. There's horse thieves around, too, so it's possible someone picked him off."

"Or he could have died of old age." Wade said, taking a sip of his water. "Isn't he one of the oldest ones here?"

"It's possible." Hank said. "That's what we need to find out. You kids ready?" He stood, having finished his burger in about three bites. "It's not getting any lighter out, you know." Virginia and Wade followed him out just as Nate, Tiff, and Emily sat down.

"Was it something I said?" Nate said innocently, looking at the three retreating backs.

"You goof." Marsha swatted his arm. "Are you seriously going to eat all that?" She pointed at Nate's burger, which he had piled four patties high with a slice of cheese between each one. In answer Nate took an enormous bite and wasn't quite able to close his mouth. Jessa had to look away. Watching people chew with their mouths open always made her want to gag. She squinted out the window to see if she could see Hank and the others ride away. Through the fog and rain she could barely make out their shapes as they passed by.

That night, Jessa pulled out her journal. She didn't write regularly, but tonight she felt enough angst that she needed an outlet.

August 3rd

Marsha and I are pretty much all set for Teepee Camp. Except, I don't want to go. I'm not at all interested in being a camp counsellor, which is basically what I will be doing. I mean sure, I can do it. I just don't want to. I'd rather stay up at the main camp, where I can hang out with Wade every day, and see Fairlight whenever I want.

I don't know if Wade likes me anymore. Anytime I try to talk to him, he's civil and polite, but there's no magic. He's turned off the chemistry somehow and treats me like we're just buddies. It's annoying. I can't wait for Virginia to leave so he will act like his normal charming self again. There doesn't seem to be much hope of getting his attention back as long as she's around. Even Nate falls all over himself when she's around. It's so pathetic. I just want things to go back to the way they were. Hopefully when I get back from Teepee Camp, Virginia will be gone and everything can be like it used to be.

Jessa Davies

CHAPTER 6
TEEPEE CAMP

The next day Jessa felt jittery. She spent the morning practicing her worship songs and felt confident that they sounded decent. She also scribbled some notes in the back of her journal with ideas for the evening devotional times, and packed her bible.

The storm had lasted most of the night, and at breakfast Hank had admitted they hadn't been able to find Chester in that weather. He hadn't been able to get ahold of the neighbours, either, so there was still a chance that Chester had strayed over there. Hank had suggested to Marsha that they take Zorro in Chester's place for Teepee Camp. He assured them he would be spending the better part of the day out looking for Chester, taking Nate's dad Fred along to help.

Before lunch, Jessa took the time to massage some serum into her dry hair and straighten it. She also applied a touch of mascara and eyeliner, finishing her look with a dab of raspberry lip balm. Looking in the bathroom mirror, she smiled, thinking her favourite pink shirt was great color on her. It brought out her glowing tan and green eyes.

With a bounce in her step, Jessa walked down to lunch. Maybe Virginia had a point. Taking the time to put in an extra effort with her appearance did make her feel more cheerful. She was certain this would get Wade's attention again.

Jessa was the last one at the table, and she squeezed in between Nate and Emily with her bowl of stew. Virginia was sitting directly across from her, and looked up with an approving smile.

"You look real pretty today, Jessa." Virginia winked.

"Thanks, Virginia, so do you." Jessa answered archly. "Where's Hank?" She said, realizing he was absent.

"Uncle is still out riding with Nate's dad." Virginia said. "He said they might be gone most of the day, looking for that missing horse."

"He's probably wearing my vest, this time." Nate said loudly. "And Chester's probably dead."

"Nate!" Emily looked up shocked. Usually she was so quiet and reserved that she didn't speak until spoken to. Jessa almost forgot she was there, half the time.

"What?" Nate said, callously buttering his hunk of bread. "It's the circle of life. Let's be realistic, here." No one responded to Nate's blunt proclamation. Jessa tried to get Wade's attention.

"So, Wade, how was your morning?" Jessa asked, dipping her chin down in what she hoped was an alluring smile. She had watched Virginia do the same motion and wanted to see if she could get Wade bantering with her again. Wade didn't seem to hear her.

"Wade?" Jessa repeated louder. He looked up with a start.

"Yeah?"

Jessa lowered her chin and looked at him through her eyelashes again. "How are you?" She repeated in a sultry voice.

"Good." He answered, looking puzzled. "Is

something wrong? Does your neck hurt?" Tiff snorted.

"No, no." Jessa straightened her head. "I was just saying hi. You know. No biggie." Her cheeks flushed, she took a sip of water and looked away. A few tables over she saw Russ standing up behind Cory-Lynn, giving her a shoulder rub. Jay was right next to them, glazing over. Jessa decided to escape from her flubbed attempt at talking to Wade, and go save Jay from his obvious discomfort. "See you guys in a bit," She said, carrying her bowl over to Jay's table.

"Is that seat taken?" She asked, nodding to the chair on Jay's far side. He looked up and beamed at her like she had just saved his life.

"Please!" Jay jumped up and pulled out the chair for her. "Thank God." He murmured to her quietly. "I don't know how much more I can take of these lovey-love-birds."

"What's that?" Russ asked. "Did I hear something about lovebirds? Cause that's totally us, isn't it Cory-boo-boo?" Cory-Lynn giggled, her cheeks bulging with food.

"You caught me." Jay threw up his hands. "I was thanking Jessa for saving me from my third-wheel meal, over here. The PDA is getting a little over-the-top, if you ask me." He gave Russ a half-serious half-joking look.

"Public displays of affection, you mean?" Russ continued massaging Cory-Lynn's shoulders. "What are you talking about? We're not making out or anything. Here, I'll show you how non-PDA this is." Russ stepped behind Jay and grabbed his shoulders, kneading them ferociously.

"Hey! Ow, man!" Jay batted Russ's hands away. "Wow, Cory-Lynn, how can you stand this guy?" He teased.

"Oh I can stand him just fine." Cory-Lynn blew Russ a kiss.

"But seriously, here." Jay said. "Can't you save some of the snuggles for the weekends off? Say, when I'm not around?"

"Sorry bro, no-can-do." Russ said just as Ms. Sheila walked over with a tray. "When it's true love, you just can't help it."

"Oh, good, just the topic I need to bring up with you two." Ms. Sheila said, placing both hands on the table and leaning over it. "The PDA. It's got to go."

"It does?" Russ looked crest-fallen. "I thought we were playing it pretty cool."

"Well, those campers by the door just asked me if you're getting married." Sheila pointed to a group of girls. "Remember what the guidebook says. They shouldn't even be able to figure out who's dating who."

"Sorry." Russ and Cory-Lynn both mumbled as Russ took his seat. Ms. Sheila sat down and sprinkled salt into her stew liberally.

"Hey, relax." She said, a twinkle in her eye. "You're not in trouble. Not much, anyway. Just keep a bible-space between you from now on, or I may have to pull rank again." Ms. Sheila held up her fingers, indicating a two-inch gap.

"You're a saint." Russ told her affectionately.

"I know." Ms. Sheila answered shortly. "Now eat your soup. Get some meat on those skinny bones."

As soon as lunch was over, Jessa's jitters tripled. She and Marsha walked over to the lodge, and in the space of a chaotic hour they had met and checked-in all of their campers.

They dropped off everyone's luggage at the lodge, then walked on to the barn. Jessa looked out over her little flock, trying to remember everyone's name. There was Brittany, a moody-looking girl with her hood-up, slouching along like this was the last place she wanted to be. Then there were three little blondes who had signed up together and were the essence of perkiness: Gracie, Ava, and Kylie. Jessa had already secretly dubbed them the 'triplets'.

Jessa already could tell that Alliyah would be the mischievous one in the group; with her impish grin and a mouth full of braces. Finally there was Wendy, who was dressed head to toe in brand-new cowboy gear, tags still dangling, and looking excited enough to jump right out of her hot-pink cowboy boots.

By the time the little troupe reached the barn, Jessa and Marsha had already been asked how old they were, whether they had boyfriends, and whether or not they thought any of the boys at camp were cute. Marsha had laughed good-naturedly and teased them.

"It's just going to be us girls at the teepees. We don't need any cute guys around to have fun, do we? Besides, boys are nasty, right, Jessa?" Marsha went on to tell them about Nate spraying juice out of his nose and taking monstrous bites out of hamburgers.

Jessa found out plenty about the girls. It turned out almost all of them had attended Spruce Ridge Camp before; except for Brittany. She had never been to camp, stating 'it's dumb' and 'my stepmother wanted to get rid of me'. To that Alliyah had fearlessly looped her arm through Brittany's and tried to get her skipping, saying 'Camp's fun, Britt! You'll love it! Do you want to ride next to me?'

The barn was fairly empty, since most of the horses and wranglers were away on afternoon trail rides. Jessa helped fit the girls with helmets, and urged them to use the outhouse while they had the chance. The blond 'triplets' made a big production of how stinky it was, and kept jumping to the back of the line. Brittany refused, saying she didn't have to go. Instead she put ear-buds in and cranked up the volume. Jessa could easily hear heavy metal music leaking out. She was just about to tell Brittany to turn it off when Marsha put a hand on her shoulder.

"What?" Jessa asked.

"Don't worry about it." Marsha suggested. "Let her

adjust in her own way. She'll come around."

"Okay." Jessa agreed. She checked the office for Hank, but there was no indication that he had returned from his search for Chester. Plus, Zorro was saddled with the other Teepee Camp horses.

Marsha gave a short pre-ride lesson, then she and Jessa helped everyone mount-up. It looked as though most of them had at least some riding experience, except for Brittany. Still, she refused help and climbed up on Zorro on her own. "I can do it myself." She glowered at Marsha.

"No problem" Marsha said easily and went to help Ava. Jessa swung up on Dusty's tall brown back, leaning forward to tousle his shaggy mane. It felt good to be back on Dusty again. Flash was okay, but there was no other horse like Dusty.

"Let's go, fillies!" Marsha hollered and led the way out of the barn gate. "And remember the three C's of horsemanship: Calm, Confidence, and Communication!" Jessa got in line last, to flank the ride.

The trail ride was leisurely and relaxing for Jessa. The 'triplets' were just behind Marsha, chattering a mile-a-minute and making Marsha laugh. Next was Brittany on Zorro, sulking, then Alliyah and Wendy. Jessa found herself making small-talk with the girls as they picked their way along the trail, weaving amongst the creamy trunks of the poplar trees; the leaves rustling in an expansive green canopy overhead.

Once they had crossed the creek and the southern-pasture, they followed a narrow trail along the edge of a steep ridge. Here there were fewer poplar trees, and more spruce trees growing close together. Jessa had never been this far away from the barn before, though she knew this was still camp property. A nearby spruce branch scratched her bare-arm as Dusty passed, leaving tiny white lines across the surface of her skin. Jessa was glad Marsha knew the way. The trail was well marked, but Jessa had lost all sense of which direction they were going.

At one point the trees were so close to the trail that Jessa had to lean forward over the saddle-horn, letting the low branches sweep over her back. She couldn't see a thing and just hoped Dusty kept following the others. At last Dusty scrambled out into a grassy meadow. Jessa felt something crawling on her and shuddered, sweeping a tiny black spider off her arm. She vigorously scrubbed her arms and legs, trying to get rid of any of his buddies. Alliyah saw her and chortled at her spider-dance.

"I got one on me, too." Wendy piped up.

"Have we got everybody?" Marsha checked. "Good. We're almost there! See where the creek winds up ahead? Just past that is the teepee!" With renewed enthusiasm the riders plodded on, coming upon the campsite in no time.

Jessa saw a large white-teepee set up in a clearing that overlooked the creek. A ring of firestones and a weathered picnic-table stood nearby, as well as a large paddock for the horses. Beyond that was an outhouse and padlocked shed. A muddy road wound away through the trees to the east.

Jessa slid off Dusty, stretching her stiff legs, and tied him to the hitching rail. Marsha was already teaching the campers how to tie a quick-release knot.

"And then we pull this loop through like this." Marsha demonstrated. "Okay, now everyone, we need to get our horses unsaddled and brushed, so we can put them in their paddock."

"But I'm too tired." Kylie whined. "And I'm hungry."

"A good horseman always takes care of his horse, first." Marsha said, and started showing them how to remove the saddle. Jessa unsaddled Dusty, and was just moving to help Wendy when she heard the rumbling of a vehicle approaching. Leaving the campers with Marsha, she trudged over to meet the truck as it pulled into camp.

"Well howdy there." Fred, Nate's dad stuck his head out the window to greet her. Nate had come along too and was riding in the passenger seat. Jessa realized for the first time how alike the father and son looked; both with black hair and brown eyes; though Fred's was cropped tidily in a militant-style, while Nate's was longer and wavy.

"Hi!" Jessa said brightly. Nate's dad had seemed stern she had first met him at the beginning of summer. But over the past weeks she had seen a more adventurous, comedic side to him.

"Hey Jessa." Nate grinned, his dark eyes crinkling at the corners. "I heard you cowgirls might want some food and sleeping bags."

"It couldn't hurt." Jessa said as Fred turned off the ignition. "Hey, Fred, did you and Hank find Chester?" Fred shook his head.

"We didn't. But we had to cut our ride short; Hank had to get back for a meeting he'd forgotten about. We're going out again tomorrow, though." Fred hopped out of the truck and walked around to the tailgate. "Nate, help me with these coolers." The men heaved the food over to the picnic-table.

"You'll want to lock these up in that shed, overnight. Keep the critters out." Fred said as Nate hauled the rest of the supplies out of the truck. Jessa saw that Nate his hoodee which he must have reclaimed from Hank, though it now appeared somewhat stretched out in the mid-section.

Jessa ducked into the teepee and was pleased to see there were several camping-foamies rolled up and stacked inside. On closer inspection Jessa thought the foamies smelled musty, but they were dry and she knew she would be grateful for them later.

"And last but not least," Fred passed her a walkie-talkie. "Here. Hank has the other one. Use it if there's any emergencies, or if you need anything. Channel three."

"Okay." Jessa said, setting it down amongst the gear on the table.

"Is there anything else you can think of that you might need?" Fred asked, climbing back into the truck.

"I don't think so. Thanks Fred. See you, Nate!" Jessa waved as the truck rambled off slowly. Jessa walked back to the hitching rail to join the campers.

"Once you've groomed your horse, go ahead and lead them into the paddock, and make sure there's plenty of food and water for them." Marsha called out. The triplets and Wendy were already untying their horses and walking them to the pen.

Jessa noticed that Zorro was still bridled and saddled, with Brittany standing next to him. Her pale face was furrowed into a scowl. Her shoulders hunched and she had shoved her hands in her sweater-pockets.

Jessa pasted on a smile and walked over to her. "Hey Brittany!" She said brightly. "How's it going?"

"This is stupid." Brittany said through clenched teeth. "I hate this."

"Okay...?" Jessa said. "I'm sorry to hear that."

"I didn't want to come here, you know." Brittany said venomously. "My evil stepmother just wanted me out of the way. I don't even like horses. And I hate camping." Jessa didn't know what to say. Marsha was busy with the other girls in the paddock. Alliyah was the only one still grooming her horse, humming as she did so.

Jessa took a step closer to Brittany. "Do you want to talk about it?" She said gently, placing a hand on Brittany's shoulder. Brittany jumped back and swatted Jessa's hand off.

"I'm not doing this. Do you get that?" Brittany raised her voice. "Just leave me alone!" Jessa was getting irritated now. Clearly the kind-and-gentle approach wasn't working here.

"That's enough, Brittany." Jessa said firmly. "It's too bad if you don't want to be here. You are here. You may as well get used to the idea. Now you untack this horse right now. He's been working hard all afternoon, and it's your job to take care of him, like it or not." Jessa realized her voice was louder than she had intended it.

"No!" Brittany yelled in her face and turned to walk away, fumbling for her ear-buds.

"Hey!" Jessa acted on instinct. She lunged forward and grabbed Brittany's arm. Brittany's eyes widened in surprise. Jessa dropped her arm at once. "You will not walk away. That's not how we do things here. If you have a problem, you face it. Now you and I are going to untack Zorro together, and then we're going to have some dinner. That's how it's going to be. Got it?"

Brittany stared at her for a full minute, as though assessing how serious she was. Finally she shrugged and turned towards Zorro. "Fine." She growled and reached for a strap on the saddle. Jessa tried to calm her breathing, and removed the bridle from Zorro's monstrous head. Neither she nor Brittany said anything for the next few minutes. Brittany made several mistakes in the unsaddling process, but Jessa decided not to say anything. As soon as the saddle was off Brittany turned to leave, but Jessa stopped her again.

"Uh-uh. Now we groom him. You brush him and I'll clean out his feet." She held out a brush inexorably to Brittany, who rolled her eyes but took it and ran it over Zorro's body.

"Now take this rope and lead him into the paddock. I'll open the gate for you." Jessa untied Zorro and passed his rope to Brittany, who shuddered a little but took it and marched to the paddock, with Zorro dawdling meekly behind. As soon as he was free Brittany stormed away, heading for the creek. Jessa saw her fling herself down against the trunk of a tree and pop her ear-buds in.

Sighing heavily, Jessa helped Alliyah put Blondie away, then walked stiffly to the picnic table. Marsha was already there, poking around in the cooler. Jessa could hear the other girls chattering away and setting up their beds in the teepee.

"How's it going?" Marsha asked.

"Don't ask." Jessa sank down and buried her face in

her hands. "I had to practically force Brittany to take care of Zorro."

"Good for you." Marsha said. "She's probably just testing the limits. I'm glad you made her do that." Marsha looked over to the creek at Brittany.

"Except now she hates me." Jessa said.

"I doubt that. She's just learned she can't push you around." Marsha shrugged. "We need to figure out dinner. These kids are going to be starving any second here." Jessa stood up and peered into the coolers.

"I'm going to be honest, Jessa. I'm a lousy cook." Marsha admitted. "How are you at the domestic arts?"

"I'm decent." Jessa said. Her mom Nancy was a nurse and did shift work, so Jessa often prepared meals for her dad and brothers.

"Thank God." Marsha said. "You can be in charge of the cooking, then."

"Unfair!" Jessa squeaked.

"I'll do dishes?" Marsha begged. "Fair trade?"

"Deal." Jessa agreed. She hated washing dishes while camping. She dug around in the bins and decided to make spaghetti and hot-dogs. Jessa got a fire crackling, which instantly drew the campers out of the teepee. They gathered around the fire, sitting on stumps. Marsha excused herself and went to invite Brittany to join them. A few minutes later the two of them joined the circle.

Jessa figured out the camp-stove and got a big pot of water boiling for spaghetti. She intended to pass out the hot-dogs and let the campers roast them over the fire. Nighttime shadows were falling fast all around them, and Jessa switched on the electric lantern. She could barely hear the babbling of the creek over the noises of the girls light-hearted bantering, the crackling of the fire, and the subtle hiss of the propane stove. Jessa stirred the pasta and swatted at a mosquito viciously, wondering where the bug-spray had gotten too. It was somewhere in the tubs, no doubt.

After dinner it was quite dark, and stars had started to appear. Jessa slipped away to find Jay's guitar and her journal while Marsha talked Wendy and Gracie into helping her with the dishes. Jessa returned to the fire just as Marsha and the girls finished heaving the food-cooler into the shed.

"Ooooh yay are you going to play?" Kylie clapped. "I love campfire songs!"

"I am." Jessa smiled. "We're going to start with one you probably all know. Marsha, you lead the actions." Jessa strummed and sang a popular worship song, while Marsha jumped around doing actions. Most of the girls joined in, except for Brittany who was gloomily staring into the fire, her hood pulled up over her head.

Oooo-Oohh, God loves me.
Oooo-Oohh, God loves you.
Oooo-Oohh God loves everybody
In the whole wide world, Oh yeah!
Stomp your feet, clap your hands,
Jump around, everybody dance!
Oooo-Oohh, God loves me.
Oooo-Oohh, God loves you.
Oooo-Oohh God loves everybody!

After three or four rowdy songs, Jessa slowed things down by plucking out an old hymn of the church, with a modern tune.

Amazing grace, how sweet the sound
That saved a wretch like me
I once was lost but now am found
Was blind but now I see.

Jessa put the guitar aside and looked around the circle. Expectant faces peered at her, illuminated by the firelight. "Great singing, guys." Jessa smiled at them.

"We're girls." Alliyah informed her, resulting in a round of sniggers.

"Girls, then. Right." Jessa said, reaching for her bible and journal. "So we're going to have a little devotional time now. Did everyone bring their bibles?" She was met with blank looks. "Okay, never mind. I'm going to share the good-news of Jesus Christ. That's what the gospel means." Over the next minutes, Jessa read through several scripture versus from the book of Romans. Bill had suggested she talk through the 'Romans Road'; several bible verses that explained what Christianity was all about.

Jessa started with Romans 3:23, 'For all have sinned and fall short of the glory of God.' She paused a moment to try to explain. "You see God is perfect, but all people are sinners."

"Except Jesus, of course." Ava piped up.

"Yes, thank you Ava. That's right, Jesus is the only perfect human there ever was." Jessa clarified.

"That's because he wasn't human." Ava declared, picking up speed. "He was really God. In a human body, obviously."

"Thanks. Okay, let's carry on," Jessa scanned her notes for the next verse. "Romans 6:23 says that 'the wages of sin is death, but the gift of God is eternal life in Christ Jesus our Lord.' That means that we deserve to die because of all the bad stuff we do. All the evil. But God gives us a free gift: salvation. Jesus died to pay for all our debt, so we can go to heaven and have eternal life. All we have to do is ask him."

"We already know all this." Kylie volunteered. "We go to church."

"Let's talk about boys!" Gracie cried.

"Oh, well maybe in a minute." Jessa fumbled with the pages. She was losing the girls' attention, fast. "Let's just finish this first." Jessa dropped the book and bent to pick it up, losing her page. The girls started chatting about which movie stars they thought were cute.

"I have an idea." Marsha said, saving her. "I'd like to tell you girls my testimony. That means how I learned about Jesus and decided I wanted to be a Christian." The girls turned to Marsha. Jessa mouthed 'thank-you'! to her.

"Okay. Here goes." Marsha threw another log on the fire, the sparks flying upwards. "Well, I grew up knowing that there was a God. My parents told me about him. But we never really went to church or anything, so I didn't give him much thought. I thought he was this strict King up in the sky who didn't really have much time of day for me." Marsha's dark skin blended in so well in the darkness that the most visible parts of her were her white teeth and hair.

"Then when I was about seven or eight years old, I went to a bible camp; a different one than this one. I didn't really have any friends there and I was kind of shy, back then. I was lonely. But my counsellor told me that God loved me and wanted me to love him back. She told me that I could ask Jesus to come live in my heart and be my best friend forever. So, I did. I felt so alive, and I knew for sure that Jesus was real."

"Since then I've grown up a lot, and now I have lots of friends and a very happy life. But my closest friend of all is Jesus." Marsha finished.

"Cool." Wendy said. "That exact thing happened to me in Sunday school when I was six."

"Me too!" Alliyah jumped in. "But it was when I was only four. My parents prayed with me."

"Let's talk about boys now!" Kylie said excitedly. "Who here has ever been kissed?"

Jessa couldn't help but chuckle. She gave up on the rest of the devotional time and let the girls talk amongst themselves while she put away Jay's guitar and straightened up the camp. The girls were still jabbering about boys when everyone was tucked into their sleeping bags for the night.

"Okay gals, I'm turning off the lantern." Marsha said. "Night night. Remember you need to wake up Jessa or me if you need to go to the outhouse or anything in the night." She clicked off the lantern, plunging the teepee into darkness. A few of the girls instantly shrieked dramatically, followed by giggles and more whispering.

Jessa tried to get comfortable on the lumpy ground. The camping foamie didn't do much to cushion her. It wasn't easy to get to sleep with the girls all chortling, either. Finally around midnight Jessa told them it was time to be quiet and get some sleep. That worked for about three minutes and then they were talking again.

"Ugh." Jessa stuffed her pillow over-top of her head and curled up in a ball, waiting for morning.

That night Jessa dreamed about Wade. In her dream Wade was riding Bea, and she was riding along beside him on Dusty. He turned to look at her, and she smiled at him. Jessa expected him to wink, or smile, or tip his cowboy hat. But instead he turned and galloped away. Jessa tried to run after him but Bea was too fast. When she finally caught up with him among the poplar trees, Virginia was there, too, riding Chester, and wearing a white wedding gown, and looking like an angel.

"Virginia? What are you doing here?" Dream-Jessa had asked as Wade took Virginia's hand, raising it to his lips to kiss it. Dream-Virginia had turned to look at Jessa with wide eyes, then opened her mouth and let out a piercing, terrified scream.

Jessa sat bolt upright in the teepee, goose bumps tingling down her neck. All was dark and quiet, except for the soft sounds of the campers breathing deeply. Jessa was drenched in sweat. Kicking off her sleeping bag, she pawed beside her bed until she found her water bottle. Uncapping it, she took a few sips, trying to calm down. The dream had seemed so real. Virginia in a white dress, holding Wade's hand, and worst of all that awful scream.

A wave of sadness rolled over Jessa. She wanted to dream about Wade holding her hand; not Virginia's. She thought of his handsome face; his deep blue eyes, his broad shoulders. She loved the way he walked; his leather chaps loosely clapping his legs with each step. Jessa remembered back to the day when Wade had looped his lariet around her waist and pulled her towards him, looking deeply into her eyes, and calling her a 'cute filly'. Now she felt achy at the thought of him spending the next three days with Virginia. Would he forget about Jessa entirely?

Despairing, Jessa rolled over. At least when she was up at camp, she could remind Wade she still existed. Now she feared he would move on and be dating Virginia by the end of the week. *It's all my fault.* Jessa thought miserably. *I should have said yes to him when I had the chance. Now it's too late.*

CHAPTER 7
MAKE YOUR LIST

Marsha and Jessa decided to let the girls sleep in the next morning while they got breakfast started. Marsha fed the horses their oats while Jessa fiddled with the knobs on the camp-stove, putting a cast-iron pan on one burner and a big pot of water on the other. Dabbing some butter in the pan to grease it, she stirred up some pancake batter. Jessa felt haggard, having slept only in snatches. She had a kink in her neck and her hair smelled like campfire smoke. She was sure if she had a mirror she would see her eyes were blood-shot.

"Horses look good." Marsha said, walking back to the picnic table. Jessa poured out four blobs of batter into the frying pan. They started sizzling and bubbling the moment they touched the hot cast-iron. Jessa grabbed a spatula and tried to flip one, but only succeeded in ripping it in half.

The first batch was a lost cause. The pancakes stuck horribly and burned, yet the insides were raw batter. Marsha hovered, concerned, no help to Jessa at all. Jessa turned the heat way down for the second batch, and they turned out perfectly. When she had a good-sized stack done, she covered them in foil and laid strips of bacon in the pan. They started to sizzle at once.

"I'll go wake the girls." Marsha said, ducking into the teepee. Jessa turned the bacon as its rich smell wafted through the air, tantalizing her. She snuck a little taste of bacon that had broken off. *I just have to make sure it's not poisonous, of course.* She thought with a sneaky smile. Jessa remembered her mom saying that same thing whenever she sampling a bit of baking before it was served.

The campers scrambled clumsily out of the teepee, wearing their pyjamas and rubbing their eyes. Kylie still had her blanket wrapped around her.

"Morning girls!" Jessa sang. "Come on over, breakfast is just about ready." She noted that Brittany was wearing the same outfit as yesterday. It appeared she hadn't bothered to change into pyjamas the night before.

Marsha said grace, then the girls dug in happily. Jessa poured steaming cups of hot chocolate into pewter mugs while the campers ate. She gave each girl a friendly smile as she passed out the mugs, thinking, *See? I can do this. I can totally be a camp counsellor.*

Later that morning, Jessa rode flank again as they took a long trail ride through the forest. Marsha led at a relaxed pace, letting the summer air warm them. On the way back to the teepee, she had everyone trot. The girls giggled and held on tight as they bounced all over the place in their saddles. Brittany even came out of her shell a little, cracking a smile at one of Alliyah's jokes.

Back at the teepee Jessa put together some sandwiches and told the girls to help themselves. She was feeling quite grubby and tired, and would have loved a shower.

"I'm going in the creek." Jessa announced. "You guys can just relax for a bit."

"I'll go too!" Alliyah jumped up, excited. "I just need to get my swimsuit on."

"Let's bring shampoo." Gracie suggested. "We can wash our hair in the creek."

"Yes! My mom got me all natural biodegradable shampoo, especially for that!" Wendy said, already heading for her bag.

"Oh, okay, I guess we'll all go, then." Jessa said slowly.

"Great idea!" Marsha beamed. Jessa didn't bother to explain that she had hoped to get some alone time. Clearly that would be impossible for the next three days.

Their time at the creek actually ended up being a lot of fun, Jessa had to admit. She bonded with the girls by showing them how to do a 'bikini-model pose' and took plenty of photos for them. The campers pranced around ridiculously, but there was no one anywhere around to see, and Jessa didn't see the harm in it. She used some of Wendy's shampoo to scrub her hair, and lay back in the cool current to let it rinse out, feeling like a nature-woman. Marsha spread her towel out on the pebbly-bank and laid back to bask. It seemed even Brittany was enjoying herself; she had finally taken off her sweater and waded in knee-deep water with Alliyah.

Jessa emerged invigorated and laid out her towel beside Marsha's, ready to lie down and bake. Marsha squinted up at her, then closed her eyes again. Jessa lowered herself onto her back and stretched out.

"So." Jessa said, "My devotions didn't go too well last night, huh?" She chuckled.

"No big deal." Marsha said. "I thought you were doing fine."

"Until I totally lost their attention and you had to jump in with your testimony. Thanks again, by the way." Jessa said.

"No problem. It looked like you needed a little help."

"They didn't seem interested in the gospel message. I

was hoping a few of them at least would have questions, want to find out about Jesus..."

"Jessa," Marsha hoisted herself up on one side and rested on her elbow. She shaded her eyes with one hand. "We aren't responsible for these girl's salvation. The best we can do is show them lots of love, and tell them the good news. Whether or not they receive it is their choice. Only the Holy Spirit can change hearts."

"I suppose." Jessa mumbled. "But now what do I do for devotions? Tonight I was going to talk about the basics of being a new Christian. Somehow I don't think any of them care about that. Most of them seem to be long-time Christians already." Marsha thought for a moment.

"Why don't we find out what they want to talk about, and go from there." Marsha suggested.

"We already know all they want to talk about is boys." Jessa said.

"Perfect." Marsha proclaimed. "We can talk about boys, and dating, and kissing, and anything else they want. From a Christian perspective. Maybe we can talk about what to look for in a guy. They'll love it."

Later that afternoon, Jessa pulled out her journal and wandered over to lounge against a tree-trunk. Mostly she just wanted an excuse to have some quiet time, and Marsha agreed to look out for the campers for a few minutes.

August 5th

Teepee Camp is going just fine. The girls seem to be having fun, which is good; even though my devotions have been a bust. At least I think the worship times are going okay. Earlier this week Jay asked me what I was going to do with my singing talents. I've considered it and I honestly don't know. I really like singing, and playing, and I'm not shy to do that in front of people. But I don't know if I feel much inclination to become a worship pastor, like him. Oh well. I guess I have a few years to decide what to do after high school.

I keep thinking about Wade. I know I'm being ridiculous, but sometimes I look up and hope he'll come riding through the trees on

Bea, to surprise visit me. Of course he hasn't. I make up these ridiculous romantic scenes, like what I've seen in movies, and it seems so real in my head. Then I realize I've been daydreaming about Wade, and wondering how I can get his attention back; rather than actually being present with the campers. It's like I'd rather chill out in my own fantasy world than actually bother to get to know them. It makes me feel like a lousy counsellor. Then again, I never asked for this role. Two more days to go.
Jessa Davies

That night after dinner, Jessa decided to take Marsha's advice. She led the girls in worship again, repeating some of the same songs she had done before. Then, she made an announcement.

"Tonight we're just going to talk about boys." Jessa said.

"Yes!" Gracie punched a fist in the air. "Finally!"

"Oh brother." Brittany rolled her eyes.

"So first things first." Kylie said imperiously. "We need the details of your past loves." She pointed at Marsha and Jessa.

"Oh, we don't need-" Jessa chuckled, shaking her head.

"Oh yes we do! Tell us everything! We deserve to know!" The campers came closer, squeezing her knees and begging for information.

"Okay, okay!" Jessa put up her hands. "Okay. Here's the scoop. I met a guy a while ago."

"Is he at the camp? What's his name?" Ava demanded.

"He's, well, let's just call him Mr. X." Jessa said. "And he's extremely handsome." The girls squealed predictably. Jessa decided to go into detail, to keep them excited. "He's tall, with these amazing blue eyes that look right into your soul, you know?" The triplets were right on the edge of their seats, eyes shining.

"He's got these really strong, broad shoulders." Jessa motioned to indicate bulky muscles. "But more importantly he's a strong Christian. He loves Jesus, and prays and reads his bible every day." Jessa cleared her throat and continued. "Mr. X is really fun to be around. He's always kind and nice, and makes me laugh."

"So, is he going to be your boyfriend?" Wendy asked hopefully. Jessa's smile faded a little.

"I don't know anymore. I used to think so. But for now we're just friends. I hope maybe one day he can be my boyfriend."

"I'm not allowed to date until I'm in high school." Wendy said glumly. "But there's a guy in my youth group I like."

"What do you ladies think is important to look for in a boyfriend?" Jessa asked, opening the conversation. Most of them jumped in and listed off physical qualities and hobbies. Marsha reminded them that a man worth being with would be one who loves Jesus first and foremost.

"The guy also needs to be respectful and polite." Marsha said. "Check how he treats his mother, and his siblings, and pets and stuff. If he doesn't treat them right, look out, cause he's on his best behaviour when he's trying to win your heart."

"Speaking of hearts." Jessa said, suddenly remembering Bill's message from earlier in the week. "The bible says we should guard our hearts."

"What does that mean?" Alliyah asked.

"I think in the case of dating, it means not giving too much of ourselves, emotionally or physically, to a man until we actually marry him." Jessa surmised. "We should protect our hearts as much as we can. No matter how much I like Mr. X, I don't know for sure if he's the one I'm going to marry. So, I need to watch it and make sure I don't let my emotions get too involved."

Even as she said it, Jessa feared her heart was already more involved with Wade than was ideal. It hadn't been until Virginia came into the picture that Jessa realized how deep her feelings really went. Marsha stepped in to add to what Jessa had said.

"I also think we should be careful not to go too far physically with a guy, until marriage." Marsha put in. "Getting too close with a boyfriend can seem exciting at the time, but it leads to all kinds of problems. If the guy really loves you and cares about you, he will respect your decision to wait."

"True love waits." Alliyah chimed in. "I learned that at youth-group."

"I may as well share my sordid history." Marsha said, breathing in deeply. Jessa sat up, paying attention. She had never heard Marsha divulge any information about past boyfriends.

"I know a guy at school, named J'Mark." Marsha said. "He's the popular guy, and I never thought he'd notice me in a million years. Well, he did. He started paying attention to me and being really nice. I thought it was the real thing. You know. Love."

"We went out to a movie one night and he kissed me, and it was the most amazing feeling. But then the next day he broke up with me and starting dated one of my friends. I found out later he just had a bet going with his friends to see if he could get the 'good-Christian-girl' to kiss him." Marsha said.

"What a jerk!" Alliyah chimed in angrily. "Did you slap him?" Marsha chuckled.

"I wanted to. But no, I was angrier with myself. I should never have handed over my heart and my lips so easily. He said all the flattering things I wanted to hear, and no guy had ever done that before. At the end of the day I wish I could take that first kiss back, and save it for someone who really deserves it; who really loves me."

CHAPTER 8
A SCREAM IN THE NIGHT

The girls proved even more reluctant to settle the second evening. It was a cool, cloudy night; Jessa couldn't see any stars in the black sky before she ducked into the teepee. The campers were far too excited to sleep, and couldn't seem to stop giggling.

Marsha came into the teepee last, having just checked the horses. "The horses seem a little restless." She said in a low voice to Jessa. "I guess they aren't crazy about being stuck in the small pen overnight."

"Yeah, I get that feeling too." Jessa smirked and gestured around the teepee. She zipped herself into her sleeping bag and stared up at the canvas walls slanting above her.

"I'm shutting off the lantern now, girls." Marsha announced. "Remember to let us know if you need to go to the outhouse or anything."

Jessa could hear the girls heckling and tickling each other. A while later she heard Alliyah whisper, "Are they asleep yet? Let's sneak to the creek and go swimming!" Both Jessa and Marsha belted, "No!" simultaneously. Jessa couldn't help but smile, as she herself had recently been guilty of the same thing; sneaking off to the creek at night for her barn-girl initiation.

Jessa closed her eyes and tried to sleep. She kept thinking about Wade. Her thoughts were half yearning, half despairing. She imagined what it would be like to be Wade's girlfriend. He certainly met all the requirements on her list. The problem was Virginia. Once Virginia was out of the picture, maybe Wade would come around and notice Jessa again. Still, the idea of being Wade's second choice wasn't exactly appealing, either.

Jessa wondered if Tiff had agonized over Wade the same way, back at the beginning of summer. Of course now Tiff had Brady to worry about. The more Jessa thought about it, the more she thought Tiff should tell Brady no, she wouldn't take him back. He wasn't a Christian anymore. Jessa remembered that the bible warned Christians about being 'unequally yoked' with an unbeliever. Jessa would tell Tiff exactly that when she saw her next.

Jessa remembered how her brother had informed her that he was still a Christian. She supposed if he still believed Jesus was his saviour, then that was true. She just didn't understand how someone who loved Jesus would purposely chase such a risky life-style. Didn't he see that his actions were not honouring to God?

Her mind whirling, Jessa finally decided to pray.

Lord, there's so much going on right now. I need your help. I have all these feelings for Wade; and I thought he liked me back, but now it seems he doesn't want me. Do I need to just step back? Let him go?

It's hard! I know you have good plans for me, and that you already know which guy I am going to end up with. It would just be really nice if it happened to be Wade, because I really like him a lot. Please reveal to me what to do. Help me guard my heart. Help me be patient and wait for the one you have for me.

Amen.

The campers were still whispering when Jessa finally fell asleep. The ground seemed to grow more comfortable, and her sleep was deep and dreamless.

A long time later, Jessa gasped and sprang up onto her hands and knees. A terrible scream had awakened her.

All was quiet in the teepee. She heard the steady breathing of the girls. Seconds ticked by, and she wondered if she had imagined the scream.

Then, coming from outside, she heard it again. All of the hairs on the back of Jessa's neck stood up at the sound of the shrill, terrified scream. With that second scream, Marsha bounded out of bed, smashing her head on the slanted teepee canvas.

"Ouch!"

"Marsha?" Jessa whispered, clutching for her. "Did you hear that scream?"

"Yes! What was that? Is it the girls?" Marsha rooted around in the dark, trying to find a flashlight.

"Did they sneak down to the creek after all?" Jessa whispered. "Maybe Alliyah's just playing a prank or something."

Marsha clicked on her light and raised the beam to look at the sleeping campers.

"No! You'll wake them up!" Jessa said, grabbing Marsha's arm.

"We have to make sure they're here." Marsha said, and Jessa let go. Marsha slowly shone the light over the sleeping campers. One, two, three, four, five were there. The sixth bed was empty.

"Brittany!" Jessa breathed in terror. "Oh my gosh Marsha!"

"We have to find her." Marsha said.

"Was that her screaming?" Jessa said, horrified.

"I don't know!" Marsha hissed. "Let's go." Marsha poked her head out of the teepee flap and swept the light beam all around the campsite.

"I don't see anything." Marsha whispered. "Come

on."

Heart pounding, Jessa followed Marsha outside. The grass was wet and cold under her bare-feet. She could barely see the outline of the picnic table, it was so dark; though a sliver of moon showed through the clouds now. A foggy mist along the ground reflected some of the light, and after a moment Jessa's eyes began to adjust.

"Brittany?" Marsha whispered hoarsely, flailing the light around. Jessa heard a horse whinnying, and the sound of hooves galloping around the small pen.

"Was it just a horse whinnying that we heard?" Jessa wondered. "Why are they running around like that?"

"I don't know." Marsha said. "I've never heard a horse scream like that. I think it was a person."

"We have to find Brittany!" Jessa said, panicking.

"But we can't just leave the other campers!" Marsha argued, pointing back to the teepee that loomed behind them.

Suddenly out of the corner of her eye, Jessa saw something dark moving in the shadows. She drew in a quick breath and instinctively clung to Marsha. Her legs felt paralyzed, rooted to the spot. For a moment her heart seemed to stop.

A dark shape was bobbing towards them, floating on the mist. Marsha dropped the flashlight in a panic, the light still on, illuminating the fog. She clutched Jessa tightly, digging her fingernails into Jessa's arm.

"Who's there?" Marsha's voice rang out, shrill.

The figure came closer. It was black and hooded. Jessa heard shuffling footsteps. Just when she was about to bolt for safety, she realized.

"Brittany?" She asked, incredulous. The person didn't answer but walked almost straight into them. Marsha grabbed the girl by her shoulders and ripped off her black hood. Instantly Brittany looked up, startled, then scowled.

"What?" Brittany yanked out her ear-buds, from which loud rock music pulsated.

"You scared us half to death, young lady!" Marsha shook Brittany's arm fiercely. "What did you think you were doing?" Brittany jerked her arm free.

"I was just in the outhouse. I needed to go to the bathroom, that's all."

"Then why did you scream like that?" Jessa demanded. Brittany looked at her blankly.

"I didn't scream."

"Yes you did!" Marsha insisted. "We heard you. That's how we realized you had snuck out. Without telling us, by the way!"

"Look, I'm telling you I didn't make a sound." Brittany said firmly. "I promise. Now can I go back to bed? It's cold out here."

"Didn't you hear screaming?" Jessa asked Brittany. "You had to have heard it. We both heard it. It was just a minute ago." Brittany shook her head and held up her earbuds.

"I had my music cranked up really loud. I didn't hear anything." Jessa and Marsha looked at each other, trying to decide whether or not to believe her.

"You guys are paranoid. I'm going to bed." Brittany announced and crouched into the teepee.

"You stay in there this time." Marsha said firmly. "And don't leave without telling us."

"Whatever." They heard her mumble as she zipped herself back into her sleeping bag. Jessa didn't know what to do next. She picked up the flashlight and again swept it over the camp, but didn't see anything unusual.

"I don't get it." Marsha finally said. "If Brittany didn't scream, well, who did?"

Jessa didn't sleep a wink the rest of the night. She and Marsha had eventually gotten back into the teepee, made sure the flap was secured shut, and laid down. She knew

Marsha didn't sleep, either. At one point she thought she heard the horses galloping again, and a dull cracking sound, followed by silence. She strained her ears, but after that all she heard was the breathing of the girls.

Jessa had left the walkie-talkie in the padlocked shed at the far edge of the paddock, and there was no way she was going over there now. Plus, what would she say if she radioed Hank? *Marsha and I heard a scream; come save us?* Jessa almost would have thought she dreamed the scream; like she had dreamed Virginia's scream the night before, except that Marsha had heard it too.

She wondered if Brittany was lying, and had been the screamer. Or maybe one of the campers in the teepee had screamed in their sleep, and it just sounded like it came from outside. Or one of the horses whinnied more high-pitched than normal.

Tossing and turning until daylight, Jessa finally sat up and looked at Marsha. "Let's go look around." She said. Marsha got up slowly as Jessa found her shoes and slipped them on. The campers were all fast asleep still as Jessa held open the flap for Marsha, then followed her out.

The morning sun shone through the trees, making the dewy grass glisten and sparkle. The creek babbled innocently, its tiny rapids gurgling past.

Jessa glanced towards the horse paddock, and her jaw dropped open. She broke into a run and in a moment was at the fence, Marsha close behind her.

The horses were gone.

"Look!" Marsha pointed. "They must have broken the fence over there. They escaped." The grey-boards had been smashed through in one area. No horses were in sight anywhere nearby.

"They could be all the way back at camp by now." Jessa said mournfully. "What are we gonna do?"

"We need to radio Hank." Marsha decided. "Where did you put the walkie-talkie?"

"In the shed." The girls raced to the old shed and

creaked the door open. Jessa dug through the supplies until she found the walkie-talkie.

"Jessa." Marsha's voice sounded strange. Jessa peeked her head out of the shed and saw Marsha looking down at the muddy road.

"What?" Jessa said, joining her.

"Look at this." Marsha pointed at the ground, her eyes wide, trembling slightly.

Jessa peered down for several seconds, not sure what she was supposed to be looking at. Then, she gasped and jumped back, clutching the walkie-talkie close to her heaving chest.

Jessa was no tracker. But there were fresh tracks in that mud, from something big. Something dangerous.

CHAPTER 9
HAVOC WREAKING

For the next hour, Jessa tried to radio Hank unsuccessfully. Either his walkie-talkie wasn't turned on, or the connection was too weak. The campers were still asleep, thankfully, and Jessa and Marsha had closed themselves back into the teepee with them.

"We aren't going anywhere until we get in touch with Hank." Marsha insisted. "It's too dangerous." Jessa agreed and tried again to radio him. All she could hear was static. Exasperated, she flung the walkie-talkie down on her sleeping bag.

"Morning." Alliyah stretched and looked up at them. Jessa pasted on a smile.

"Hi! How'd you sleep?" She asked.

"Good." Alliyah said. Just then Jessa thought she heard a noise outside. She cocked her head, trying to hear. It sounded like a running vehicle, and it was coming closer.

"It's the truck!" Jessa scrambled outside. The truck pulled up close to the picnic table and the door opened. Jessa had never been more relieved to see Hank in her life. She ran at him, talking a mile a minute. Nate hopped out of the passenger seat, looking relieved to see her.

"I've been trying to reach you!" Jessa blurted out. "The horses are gone, and we saw tracks-"

"I know the horses got out. They were waiting outside the barnyard this morning, covered in sweat." Hank said gravely.

"They ran all the way back?" Jessa asked. Hank nodded.

"There's something else, Jessa." He said. "I'm afraid I have some hard news."

"What?"

"It's Dusty." Hank said. "He was attacked last night."

"Attacked?" Dread rose up in Jessa's throat. "By what?"

"A cougar." Hank said. "Dusty made it back to the barn, but he's hurt pretty bad Jessa. It's not looking good."

"No!" Jessa cried, scared at the look in Hank's eyes.

"I'm so sorry, Jessa." Hank said. "I know how much Dusty means to you. The vet is on his way over now."

"I have to see him." Jessa said, her vision blurring. Nate stepped forward hesitantly and held out his arms. Jessa collapsed on her friend's shoulder.

"It's okay." Nate patted her back and let her cry.

"I'm going to take you all back up to camp right now." Hank said. "These campers can finish up their week at the lodge. It's just not safe to be out here when there's a cougar prowling around."

The next hour passed in a daze. Somehow Hank and Marsha got all the campers and gear loaded in the back of the truck. Jessa and Nate sat in the cab. She vaguely heard Hank say that they had finally found Chester's remains the day before; he had clearly been the cougar's first victim.

"I didn't worry too much about it, at first." Hank said. "These things happen. Predators need prey; and unfortunately sometimes they turn to domestic animals. What worries me is that this cougar hasn't moved on. Normally they have a huge territory, and are transient. But this one seems to be sticking around."

"There were tracks at the campsite this morning." Jessa mumbled, sniffling. She clutched at the armrest for support as Hank swerved around a mud-hole.

"I just thank God that none of you girls were hurt."

"I heard it scream in the night." Jessa shivered at the recollection. "Right when one of our campers was outside. If anything had happened to her…"

"Clearly God was watching out for her." Hank said gently. "I've radioed Ms. Sheila and told her to keep all the campers indoors for now, and cancel all the regular activities. I have a wildlife expert coming later on to do an investigation."

Hank dropped off Marsha and the campers at the lodge, then drove Jessa and Nate on to the barn. As soon as they arrived Jessa bolted inside.

"Wait! You might not want to see..." Nate's voice trailed off as Jessa stopped short at the box stall. Dusty lay in the straw, quivering and struggling to get up. A thin man in a lab-coat was kneeling over him, giving him an injection in the neck. Jessa felt sick at the sight of her beloved Dusty; long claw-marks raked into his neck and back, and his head covered in blood.

"Dusty." Jessa whispered, her eyes filling again. Nate stood behind her and placed a comforting hand on her shoulder.

"How's he doing?" Hank said. Jessa hadn't noticed him standing next to her.

"Not great." The vet said shortly. "I've just given him some medication to help him relax and numb the pain. We need to make a difficult decision here, though."

"What does he mean?" Jessa choked, looking from the vet to Hank. "He's going to be okay, isn't he?"

"It's not looking good, Jessa." Hank said, his eyes locking on hers.

"What are you saying?" She cried. The vet answered simply.

"The kindest thing at this point would be to put him down."

"No!" Jessa sobbed, burying her face in her hands. How could this have happened? It was horrific. It was unfair. She loved Dusty so much; he meant the world to her. How could he come to such a horrible end?

"He's in pain, Jessa." Hank said quietly.

"He's an old horse, too." The vet said. "It would be a hard, long recovery, if he were to make it. It would mean a lot of stitches and antibiotics and rest, and even then he might not survive." Dusty laid his shaggy brown head down in the straw and closed his eyes, letting out a loud sigh.

"Why is he doing that?" Jessa said, hearing the panic in her voice.

"It's just from the medication." The vet said. "It's helping him relax, that's all." Jessa crouched down at Dusty's head and reached out to pat him. She could smell the sweat and blood as she bent nearer, running her hand gently over his nose. It felt like velvet. Dusty gave a weak grunt at her touch.

"Well, Hank?" The vet said expectantly.

"Let's talk in my office." Hank motioned for the vet to follow him. "Will you be okay to stay with Dusty for a few minutes, Jessa?"

"I'll stay with her." Nate volunteered, kneeling down to rub Dusty's flank. Jessa attempted a grateful smile at Nate but the tears flooded her eyes again.

Over the next several minutes Tiff, Wade, and Virginia all stopped by the box stall. Jessa didn't bother trying to hide her tears from them, and let Nate do most of the talking. She wished they would just go away. She knew they meant well but she didn't even hear the words they offered. Eventually her well-meaning friends went back to their work; leaving her and Nate alone with Dusty again.

"I'm so sorry this happened, Jessa." Nate finally said.

"I'm sure this is so hard for you."

"Thanks Nate." Jessa said. "You've been so supportive."

"Sure." Nate said, smoothing Dusty's brown hair, avoiding the bloody scratches.

"Jessa." Hank said from the stall door, making her jump. Jessa already knew what he was going to say. He walked closer and knelt beside her, resting his calloused hand on Dusty's neck.

"I'm sorry, Jessa." Hank said. "But we need to let Dusty go." Jessa had no words, only tears. She kept her hand on Dusty's warm nose.

"Do you want to wait in the office? I'll come with you." Nate offered. Jessa shook her head, wiping her nose on her sleeve.

"I want to stay with him." She said brokenly. Hank nodded to the vet. Jessa couldn't watch as the vet prepared a syringe, then knelt beside her. Jessa's throat felt so heavy and choked she couldn't say more. There were things she wanted to say to Dusty, but she couldn't get enough air. If she could have, she would have told him what a good boy he was, and how brave and strong. She would have thanked him for teaching her to ride. She would have said she would never forget him, and he would always be in her heart. She would tell him goodbye.

Jessa stroked his nose gently. She hoped that somehow he would understand what her heart wanted to say, but couldn't. She was barely aware of Hank and Nate kneeling next to her in the yellow straw.

"He won't feel anything." The vet said as he leaned forward to give the injection.

In the space of a few minutes, it was all over. Dusty was gone forever.

CHAPTER 10
BLISSFUL OBLIVION

Looking back, Jessa could never quite remember what happened right after Dusty died. She knew at some point Hank called her parents to come pick her up. Jessa had protested, not wanting to leave Marsha in the lurch with the campers. Hank had insisted, saying she needed to take a day or two off and rest.

Nate had gone with Jessa back to camp, and waited with her in the parking lot. By then Jessa thought she had no more tears, but as soon as her mom's truck pulled in, her face crumpled again. Nancy had held her and rocked her while she sobbed like a baby.

It was a sweet relief to stumble into her own messy room at home, the mid-day sun pouring through the window and warming her bed. Jessa sunk under the quilt and was asleep the moment her head touched the pillow; drifting into blissful oblivion.

Jessa slept hard and long. It wasn't until the next morning that she opened her eyes. She rolled onto her side and saw a beautifully prepared tray on her bedside table, complete with a juice box, a plate of oatmeal cookies, and a bunch of fragrant sweet peas from her mother's garden. Jessa reached for the snacks and ate them in bed, feeling like a queen. The room was so still she could see tiny particles floating through the air, all along the sunbeams that shot through the window.

Jessa's whole body felt relaxed, and her heart felt much more peaceful than it had yesterday. The piercing shock of losing Dusty had gone, leaving in its place a dull ache. Still, she felt calm now. One of her favourite bible verses came into her mind at that moment, from Psalm 23. 'Even though I walk through the valley of the shadow of death, I will fear no evil, for you, oh Lord are with me, Your rod and your staff comfort me." Jessa had walked through that valley with Dusty yesterday.

Slowly pushing back the quilt, Jessa sat up to look outside. Kenny was riding his bike in the driveway while her dad mowed the lawn. Aurelia was prancing around Kenny, her tail wagging exuberantly.

Jessa treated herself to a nice hot bubble bath, then dressed in clean clothes and went downstairs.

Clark and Nancy were sitting together in the kitchen. They both stood when she entered.

"Hi honey. Did you sleep okay?" Nancy gave her a tight snuggle. "Let me get some toast for you."

"Yes I did." She said as Clark leaned over to give her an awkward hug.

"Sorry to hear about your horse, Jess. That really sucks." Clark said.

"Thanks Clark." Jessa said, relieved he wasn't trying to make any insensitive jokes.

"Hank called this morning." Nancy said, spreading peanut butter on Jessa's toast and passing it to her. "He said there were a few more horses missing, now." Jessa's head jerked up in surprise.

"Who?" Jessa demanded. "Which horses?"

"I don't know." Nancy shrugged. "I didn't ask. Hank said the wranglers are riding out this afternoon to look for them. They're taking some specialist-wild-life guy along to investigate, too."

"I need to go." Jessa jumped up, spilling her milk. "I should help them."

"Oh, honey." Nancy put a hand on Jessa's shoulder. "Why don't you just stay home a while. You've had quite a traumatic experience. I'm sure they can manage without you." Clark grabbed some paper-towels to clean up the spill.

"No, I need to be there." Jessa said determinately, already pulling on her cowboy boots. "I have to do this. For Dusty." A lump rose up in her throat but she swallowed it back down, grabbing her coat off the hook. "It's important to me, mom. Plus, I should probably say goodbye to my campers before they go. It's Saturday; their parents are picking them up after lunch. I'm supposed to be the counsellor."

Jessa felt a twinge of guilt, knowing she hadn't done a very good job at that role. She had missed half of their week, and when she had been there she wasn't the most enthused about it.

"I'm sure they can manage without you, Jess. You have to give yourself some time."

"Mom, I have to. I'll just go for today; to say goodbye to my campers, and help find the missing horses. Then I'll come home. I'll, I'll even stay home for the rest of the summer." Jessa said with resolve.

"What?" Clark said. "You'd really quit? But you love working at camp."

"Not anymore." Jessa shook her head. What was left for her there? She had lost Dusty, she had lost Wade, and she was a lousy counsellor. "There's nothing there for me anymore."

Nancy looked at her for a long moment, considering what she'd said.

"I think you should just let her do what she wants, mom." Clark said flatly. Jessa stared at him. He had never been one to fight in her corner before. "Jessa's old enough to know how she wants to live her life. I think you should trust her. Let her go."

"Stay out of this, Clark." Nancy said, irritated lines creasing her forehead.

"Thanks, bro." Jessa gave her brother a grateful head-tilt.

"No problem. Does this mean you'll introduce me to your hot friends?" Clark grinned playfully.

"No!" Jessa said, trying to keep from smiling. "Mom, please. It's important to me. Just let me finish the week well, and say my goodbyes. Please." After a terse silence, Nancy gave in.

"Okay." She finally said. "As long as you're sure you want to go back."

"I am." Jessa said. "For one last ride."

CHAPTER 11
MAKING THINGS RIGHT

Jessa arrived back halfway through lunch. The dining hall was loud and messy, as usual. She thought she smelled tacos but wasn't remotely hungry. Marsha and the Teepee Camp campers were all sitting together near a window. Taking a deep breath, Jessa walked that way. She passed by the support staff table and dodged Russ's flailing, bony elbow; he and Cory-Lynn were tussling in the middle of an aggressive thumb-war.

As soon as they noticed her, Alliyah and the triplets all sprang up and gave her clingy hugs, acting like she was their long-lost big sister.

"Jessa we missed you so much!" Gracie pouted, pulling her by the hand to sit down. "It was so sad that your favourite horse died. I cried."

"Me too!" Kylie added.

"Thanks, you guys." Jessa took her seat. Even Brittany looked somewhat pleased to see her. At least, she wasn't scowling. Jessa saw that Brittany and Alliyah were wearing matching friendship bracelets of bright, braided threads.

"Aren't you eating anything?" Marsha asked.

"I ate before I came." Jessa said.

"It's so scary that there's a cougar out there." Kylie shuddered and looked over her shoulder out the window, almost as if she expected to see it prowling. "It's pretty much like a lion, right? I can't believe it ate your favourite horse!"

"Maybe it's for the best, though." Wendy said. "He was old, right? At least one of the younger ones didn't get eaten."

"Wendy!" Marsha tried too late to stop her. The tender wound in Jessa's heart felt raw, and she set her jaw, willing herself not to say anything in response.

"The good thing is, there's lots of other horses you can ride instead." Ava said, clearly trying to be helpful.

"Yeah! You know, Peaches is really sweet." Kylie jumped in. Jessa didn't know how much more she could take of this. She was just about to excuse herself and escape when Brittany spoke up. Her voice was softer than Jessa had ever heard it.

"Um, Jessa?" Brittany said. "Can we talk privately?" Jessa rose wordlessly and followed the younger girl. Brittany led her outside, and sat down at one of the sunny picnic tables outside the dining hall. Jessa sat down. Already parents were arriving, and helping their kids haul backpacks and sleeping bags to the parking lot.

"What's up?" Jessa said, avoiding Brittany's gaze. The last thing she felt like doing was hearing anything Brittany had to say. It wasn't as though they had exactly hit it off at the camp-out.

"I was hoping you'd come back." Brittany said, fidgeting. "I had some stuff I wanted to say to you."

"Okay." Jessa scooped up a twig off the ground and started peeling off its bark. "Let's hear it."

"It's just this." Brittany took a deep breath. "I wanted to say I'm very sorry. That Dusty died. Marsha said he was very special to you." Jessa was so surprised she couldn't speak. The air around her seemed thin.

"I know how hard it is to lose someone you care about." Brittany continued. "And I know nothing I say will make the pain go away. I just wanted to say I'm sorry for your loss, and if you want to talk about it, well, I'm here."

"Brittany!" Jessa's hand flew to her mouth, shocked tears forming in her eyes. "Thank you so much."

"I guess when it comes to this stuff, I know what to say." Brittany stated.

"How?" Jessa asked.

"My grandpa died last year." Brittany said, studying her hands. "It was terrible. He was actually in an accident, and hung on for a couple days. Then after"- Brittany paused a moment and swallowed. "After he was gone, so many people tried to comfort us. I know they meant to help. But sometimes those feel-better phrases just make things worse. All I needed people to say was that they were sorry, and that they were there for me. The other comments aren't exactly helpful."

"You are so right." Jessa said, still feeling the sting from some of the comments around the lunch-table.

"Also." Brittany ploughed on. "I owe you an apology."

"For what?" Jessa asked.

"For acting like a spoiled jerk the first couple days here." Brittany said. "I had just had a fight with my stepmother, and I took it out on you. That wasn't right. It wasn't the Christian thing to do."

"Are you a..." Jessa started in surprise, then stopped herself.

"A Christian?" Brittany asked, grimacing. "Yes I am. I feel terrible that you didn't know that. I know I wasn't exactly acting like a Christian should. There's that song; 'And they'll know we are Christians by our love?' I really messed up with that this week. I'm sorry."

"I messed up, worse." Jessa said, putting a hand on Brittany's arm. "I don't think I was a very good counsellor,

Brittany. I should have spent more time trying to get to know you. I see now what an amazing girl you are, and I missed my chance."

"It's okay." Brittany placed her hand over Jessa's. "Let's forgive each other. And I'll try not to be such a big nightmare when I come back to camp next year, okay?" Both girls laughed. The bell rang, making them both jump.

"My parents will be here soon, I think." Brittany said. "Can I pray for you, Jessa?"

"You blow me away." Jessa said, staring at Brittany in awe. Brittany laughed again and, keeping her hand on Jessa's, prayed aloud.

"Dear Lord, please comfort Jessa right now. She's really hurting, and it's been so hard for her to lose Dusty like this. Put the right people in her path that she can talk to, and who can comfort her. We know how much you love her, Lord. Help her feel your presence. Encourage her, Father. And thank you, for protecting us at the camp-out. We know nothing happens unless it's part of your plan, Father, and I know you were keeping us safe that night. Thank you. We pray this in Jesus name, Amen."

Jessa wiped her tears away, feeling a quiet peace settle on her. She leaned forward to give Brittany a tight hug.

"You're an amazing girl, Brittany." Jessa whispered in her ear.

"Britt!" A male voice called. Jessa pulled away and saw a smiling, bow-legged man ambling over. He was holding hands with a squat, Asian woman.

"Dad!" Brittany gave her dad a hug, then her stepmother. "This is my counsellor, Jessa. She protected me from the cougar."

"Oh, I didn't really do-" Jessa started. Brittany's dad squeezed her into a tight hug before she could say another word, lifting her feet off the ground and compressing all the air out of her lungs. "Ooof!" Jessa said as she returned to earth.

"Thank you so much for protecting our daughter."

He said sincerely.

"Of course." Jessa rubbed her ribs. "Anytime."

"Will you write me, Jessa? I gave Marsha my address." Brittany asked.

"Sure. I will." She promised.

"Bye!" With that Brittany walked away, her parents sandwiching her in between them.

CHAPTER 12
SEARCHING

After all the campers had left, Jessa and Marsha walked down to the barn together, and Jessa told her what had happened with Brittany.

"You know," Marsha said, "She was like a different camper after you left yesterday. Totally."

"I know." Jessa said. "Here I thought she would be the last person in the world to become a Christian. I feel so dumb now. She was already a believer the whole time; and probably a stronger Christian than I am."

"This just proves," Marsha said. "We don't know what's really going on in someone's head. 'Man looks at the outward appearance, but God looks at the heart.'"

"She prayed for me." Jessa said. "I feel so humbled. She ministered to *me*. I thought it was supposed to be the other way around. I had such a bad attitude about leading Teepee Camp in the first place. I was so selfish. So focused on me and what I wanted. I didn't even want to go."

"The Lord works in mysterious ways." Marsha said as they reached the barn. Jessa saw that most of the herd was in the paddock, with the gate closed. Nate and Emily sat

91

on the top rail overlooking the horses, and waved at Jessa as she arrived.

"Hank wants at least two people to stand guard over the herd, until the cougar moves on." Marsha told her. "He even put the mares and foals and the driving team in the main pen."

Jessa walked into the barn and avoided looking at the box stall, where Dusty had died. She couldn't bear to see the blood on the floor. Hank and Tiff stood in the tack-room, talking to a stranger. Jessa supposed he was the expert who would be coming on the search.

"Jessa!" Hank hugged her gingerly. "You're back. How are you holding up?"

"Okay." Jessa mumbled as Tiff squeezed her shoulder. She didn't want to look directly at Hank. "But Hank, I, I don't think I can work here anymore." She found she couldn't keep the words in. She hadn't planned to say them that way; they just tumbled out. "Dusty's gone, and, I just don't think I can stay."

"Oh Jessa." Hank said, his voice heavy.

"I'm okay." Jessa repeated, staring at the ground. "I want to help find the missing horses. But that's all."

"You can't just leave!" Tiff spouted, her dark brows drawing together. "Hank, tell her!"

"It's her decision, Tiff." Hank said. "But let's talk about this later. Right now, we have to worry about Brutus and Fairlight." Jessa's head snapped up, the color draining out of her face.

"Fairlight?" She whispered, staring into Hank's lined face.

"You didn't know?" Hank's eyes widened in surprise. "It's Fairlight and Brutus that are missing. They didn't come in with the herd this morning. I meant to keep the herd shut up in the pen overnight, but Virginia didn't know that and she let them out to pasture."

"No!" Jessa yelled, the volume shocking even her. She wanted to scream. Not Fairlight. Anyone but Fairlight.

Jessa heard a silky laugh through the closed office door. She didn't think. She spun on her heel and flew to the office. Throwing the door open, she saw Wade and Virginia sitting close on the bench, his arm around her. They both looked up in surprise.

Jessa bounded straight up to them, ignoring the startled look on Virginia's pretty face. In her minds' eye she saw Fairlight's beautiful golden body, lying broken in a pool of blood.

"You promised you would look after her!" Jessa screamed, her eyes squeezing shut. She couldn't look at Wade. "You promised you would take care of Fairlight for me! How could you let them out? How could you!" Jessa flung her arm over her eyes, choking back a sob. Virginia and Wade had both jumped to their feet and were talking at the same time.

"I'm so sorry Jessa! I didn't realize we were supposed to keep the herd in till it was too late. I made a mistake. I feel awful. I'm so sorry. You have to believe me." Virginia begged.

"It wasn't her fault Jessa." Wade said.

"Shut up!" Jessa screeched at him. "Just shut up, Wade!"

"Jessa!" Tiff and Hank had followed her in, and now Hank put a firm hand on her shoulder. "I know you're really hurting right now. But this isn't helping. We need to ride out and find her. There's still a chance."

"There's no hope." Jessa said, shrinking at the thought.

"As long as there is life, there is hope." Hank said. "Now get Flash. We're going." Jessa stormed out of the office and launched herself onto Flash's back. Marsha had climbed up on Jinx and looked at her timidly.

"Jessa, are you okay?"

"No!" Jessa lashed out. "Why didn't you tell me it was Fairlight? We should have left hours ago!"

"Brutus is gone, too." Marsha said weakly. "I thought

someone had told you."

"Well, they didn't." Jessa snarled as Hank, Tiff, and the investigator mounted and trotted over. "Aren't the lovebirds coming?" Jessa scowled.

"Everyone else is staying here to keep an eye on the herd." Hank said. "Jessa, this is Lorne. He's an experienced wildlife officer, and he's helping us out." The grizzled cowboy riding Leviathan was dressed head-to-toe in leather, and his face looked leathery too. "Let's go!"

Jessa kicked Flash into a run, and a moment later the riders were out the barn gate and charging towards the creek.

"We'll start by combing the pasture." Hank yelled. "Then we'll follow the creek from there."

Jessa stopped at the creek, sweeping her gaze up and down the banks for any sign of the horses.

"We need to slow it down a notch, Jessa." Hank said. "And quiet down. Let Lorne look for clues." Jessa sighed impatiently as Lorne dismounted and looked carefully at the mud and the creek-banks. His eyes squinted as he reached down to touch the earth. Wordlessly he climbed back on Leviathan, and walked him through the creek.

Jessa followed, feeling the water splash her jeans. A cloud moved over the afternoon sun, shading the creek. Lorne took the lead, walking Leviathan calmly up the far creek-bank and through a grove of young poplars. Jessa stayed close behind him, twisting all around in the saddle to look in every direction. At one point she thought she saw something silver glint from Lorne's saddle, near his knee, but then it was gone, concealed by his fringed chaps.

Lorne took his time, stopping every so often to look at the forest floor and the trees. Jessa had no idea what he was looking for. His slow pace irritated her. Shouldn't they be splitting up to find Fairlight? Every minute they poked around there was a greater chance they'd find her dead. Didn't anyone understand that?

"This way." Lorne croaked, his low voice making

Jessa jump. Her thoughts were so crowded she hadn't realized how quiet the forest was.

Lorne pushed his way through a bushy copse of spruce trees and continued on up the creek. They were further north than Jessa had ever ventured on the camp property; though technically this land was still part of the grazing pasture.

Once through the spruce, Flash snorted loudly and stopped still.

Lorne held up a hand, silently motioning for everyone to halt. Then, he placed a finger on his lips, telling them to be quiet. The forest grew thick here; a mix of mature poplar-trees, spruce and pines. Then, Lorne made eye contact with Hank, and pointed straight down.

Jessa looked where Lorne was pointing, squinting to see it clearly in the shadow of Leviathan. A fresh cougar print was pressed in a pool of mud. The edges of the track were still ever so slowly moving; sinking inwards.

A blood-curdling scream sliced through the air. It seemed to come from right under the horses' feet. Tingles shot down Jessa's spine and her ears rang; her breath stopped.

Flash leapt in the air in an almighty rear. Jessa wasn't ready for it; she clutched for the saddle-horn, but Flash was already turning in mid-air. Jessa somersaulted backwards off Flash's rump and landed flat on her back in the mud.

From where she lay, Jessa saw something move in the treetops. She couldn't breathe. She couldn't think.

Out of the corner of her eye, Jessa saw Hank lunge for Flash's reigns and hold him fast, though he struggled and pulled. Lorne moved quickly, holding up something silver. Jessa heard a twang, and a whoosh of something zing through the air. Somehow the sound triggered her breathing reflex. Jessa gasped, filling her lungs with air; not enough though. Her eyes were still fixed on the treetops.

Something was rustling the branches. Leaves fluttered down, and a shower of pine needles. Then, something heavy was falling, cushioned by the many branches, thumping from branch to branch, and finally landing out of sight on the other side of the trees.

"Did you get it?" Hank asked Lorne. Jessa sprang up, dripping in mud. Hank had looped Flash's reigns over his saddle horn, and had his finger ready on a can of pepper-spray.

"We got her." Lorne said, lowering the long, silver barrel of a gun.

"Did you kill-?" Marsha began. Lorne shook his head.

"Tranquilized." He said." This cougar's just a young thing; probably it's her first year out on her own. Trying to figure out how to survive."

"So she's just asleep?" Jessa asked, uneasy about being the only one on the ground with the cougar nearby.

"She'll be out for a couple hours, at least." Lorne said, dismounting. "I'll take her far out into the mountains where she can't hurt nobody. You wanna see her?"

Jessa shook her head as Hank radioed up to the camp, telling Fred where to bring the truck and cougar-cage. Lorne intended to stay with the sedated cougar while the rest of them rode on, looking for Fairlight and Brutus.

Jessa climbed back up on Flash, feeling shaky. Her backside was caked with mud. "Thanks a lot, Flash." Jessa grumbled irritably. "Get goin'."

Jessa, Hank and Marsha continued on, following the creek further north. Where the camp property ended, Hank turned west to continue along the cut-line. Jessa saw no sign of Fairlight or Brutus anywhere.

They came to a boggy clearing and slogged through it; Hank in the lead to pick the safest route. Flash was unruly and frankly Jessa couldn't blame him. Jessa kept a firm reign and urged him to follow.

Beyond the clearing, Jessa spotted a huge thicket of tangled brush. It would be impossible to ride through; the growth was so dense. Hank stopped a moment and pondered, stroking his white beard.

"We'll need to go around." He said, when suddenly Flash perked up his ears towards the thicket. His nostrils flared and he let out a short, fast breath, like a puff. Jessa thought she heard something deep in the thicket. A nicker.

"Fairlight!" Jessa yelled, leaping out of the saddle and running towards the thicket. "Fairlight! FAIRLIGHT!" There was nothing.

Then, closer, a high-pitched whinny answered Jessa's call.

"Fairlight! This way! Over here!" Jessa yelled. There was a crashing sound, like hundreds of tiny branches being trampled out of the way. Then, almost before Jessa dared to hope, Fairlight burst out of the thicket, with Brutus hot on her heels.

Fairlight barrelled towards Jessa, whinnying and bucking excitedly. She stopped just before colliding with her, and was whinnying, prancing, sniffing, and nuzzling Jessa all over. Jessa threw her arms around Fairlight's neck, drinking in the sight of her. She had never seen a more beautiful horse in the world.

Fairlight was covered in mud, and had a few scratches and nicks, but appeared unharmed otherwise. Brutus looked about the same. Marsha climbed off Jinx and scrubbed Brutus's forehead, crooning to him.

"Looks like they're just fine." Hank said. "They must have been separated from the herd; but they stuck together and the cougar didn't catch them. Thank you Jesus!" He passed Jessa a rope and she looped it around Fairlight's neck.

"Come on, sweetie." Jessa stroked Fairlight's golden coat, and ruffled her thick black mane. "We're taking you home."

CHAPTER 13
LET GO

Back at the barn, Jessa fed Fairlight a sweet-feed oat mix, and sponged her all over with warm water. She even shampooed her mane and tail, and cleaned her dainty black feet. Fairlight kept craning her head around to nuzzle Jessa, her black eyes soft and glowing.

"I missed you too, sweetie." Jessa snuggled her and combed out her wet mane. Then, she ran her hands over Fairlight's curved back, marvelling at how perfect she was.

"She really is a pretty horse." Virginia's silvery voice floated through the corridor. Jessa looked and saw her standing there, looking immaculate as ever in black jeans and a vest. Virginia stepped closer and patted Fairlight's nose.

"I guess I owe you an apology." Jessa said. "I shouldn't have lost it on you in the office like that."

"It's alright." Virginia said kindly. "You've been through a lot."

"Thanks, Virginia." Jessa said, forcing a civil smile. "Are you coming to the staff chapel tonight?"

"Oh, no I'm afraid I already have plans." Virginia said, smoothing back her blond curls. "Wade and I are going out for dinner in Sun Valley."

Jessa felt as though she had been punched in the stomach. They were actually going on a real date. They were dating. "I see." She managed and turned back to Fairlight, leaning on her for support. "Well, have fun with that."

"Again, I'm sorry for letting Fairlight out to pasture. And hey, if you ever want to talk..."

"Thanks, I'll keep that in mind." Jessa said, knowing she would never confide in Virginia. Jessa watched her walk back into the barn, and saw Wade slip his lariet around Virginia's waist and pull her towards him, her lilting laugh ringing through the air.

It hurt. Jessa buried her face in Fairlight's mane, breathing in deeply, smelling her. Her heart felt splintered. She didn't want to see Wade ever again. She felt she had, to some extent, opened her heart to him and put herself out there, and he had rejected her for someone else.

Jessa's logical side reasoned that she had been the one to reject Wade, weeks ago when he wanted to ask her out. She had still hoped he might keep pursuing her, even so. That hadn't happened.

Jessa put Fairlight back in the paddock and kissed her on the nose. Then, she slipped away from the barn without saying anything to anyone. She needed some time alone.

Walking back to the lodge, Jessa felt detached, blind to the forest's late afternoon beauty. The mulch crunched under her cowboy boots.

Her lodge room was empty. Someone had brought her Teepee Camp stuff in and dumped it on her bed. Jay's guitar was there, too, and her journal. She flipped through it, skimming her last few entries. She didn't feel ready to write about what had happened to Dusty. Not yet.

Jessa picked up the guitar instead, and settled into her

lower-bunk, her back against the wall. She picked out a few tunes, playing with the melodies and chords. Then, a new song poured out from her heart. When she finally looked up at the clock, she saw she had missed dinner and chapel was to start in a half hour. Jessa stood and stretched, picking up Jay's guitar. She needed to return it to him.

Jessa walked over to the chapel, avoiding the dining hall. She didn't feel ready to face her friends, yet. She could say her final goodbyes to them after chapel; just before her mom picked her up.

Jessa pushed open the weathered door and breathed in the chapel's familiar musty scent. It was all lit up inside, and Jay stood near the front, hooking up microphone chords. He saw her at once and smiled.

"Jessa." He said. "If it isn't my favourite wrangler." Jessa walked up to the front, holding out Jay's guitar.

"I need to give this back to you." Jessa said.

"Why don't you hold onto it for the rest of the summer?" Jay offered, plugging in an amplifier.

"I'm not staying the rest of the summer." Jessa said. "My mom's picking me up after chapel." Jay stopped and looked up at her.

"You're leaving?" He looked disappointed. Jessa nodded.

"Thanks for the loaner, though. It worked out great. I even wrote a song with it."

"No kidding." Jay said. "I need to hear that."

"No, I don't think I'm ready to share it." She said shyly.

"Come on." Jay urged. "I really want to hear it. Consider it a fair payment for the guitar loan." Jay settled himself down on the front pew and rested both arms across the back. "I'm ready." He grinned.

"Fine." Jessa rolled her eyes, smiling. "Just don't judge me. I don't know if this is any good." She started strumming softly.

I'm singing this song to say goodbye
To let you know I'm moving on
I have to at least try.
I can't keep you close, can't hold you tight.
I'm letting you go, tonight.
It wasn't my choice, I hope you know
But I'm letting you go, tonight.
I'm moving on, because that's what's right.
It won't be easy but I can't fight.
I'm letting go, tonight.
Walking on, tonight.
Letting you go, tonight.

Jessa finished and looked at Jay. He seemed stunned as he sat forwards and rested his elbows on his knees.

"That. Was. Amazing." Jay articulated. "Beautiful."

"Thanks." Jessa blushed and passed the guitar to him.

"Was that about the horse? The one who died yesterday?" Jay asked gently. Jessa paused, considering how much to divulge. Then, she decided to be open. She would likely never see Jay again anyway, after tonight.

"Partly." Jessa answered, sitting down on the pew next to Jay. "It's also about a guy. I liked him a lot, and I thought he liked me back. But now he's going out with someone else."

"Ah." Jay said sagely. "That's hard."

"Yes." Jessa said. "I was upset about that all week, and I wanted to get him back. Now I feel like an idiot."

"Hey." Jay looked into her eyes. Jessa had never noticed that his eyes were green, like hers. "You shouldn't beat yourself up. Let me tell you something, Jessa. It's important, so listen carefully, okay?" Jessa nodded.

"You're an amazing girl. God already knows what lucky guy you're going to end up with." Jay said firmly. "This guy you like? It sounds like he's not the right guy for you. That's obvious to me. If he was so quick to drop you and chase after someone else, that should tell you

101

something. Bless his heart." Jay added with a wry grin.

"The right guy will pursue you. He'll romance and woo you, and do whatever it takes to win your heart. He won't even notice any other girls because you'll be the only one he can imagine being with. You'll never have to try to 'get him back' or win back his affection. Remember 1 Corinthians 13? Love is patient. True love will wait, and last a lifetime. And that's the kind of guy, and the kind of love, you should hold out for. Okay?"

"Okay." Jessa said softly, touched. She couldn't look away from his kind face.

"I feel kind of sorry for the sorry-sap who let you get away." Jay chuckled. "He must not exactly be the sharpest knife in the drawer, poor soul." Jessa snorted with laughter and clapped a hand over her mouth.

The chapel doors burst open and the camp staff poured in, talking and laughing. Jessa said goodbye to Jay and joined her friends, sitting between Tiff and Marsha.

"I made a decision. About Brady." Tiff leaned closer to her. "I sent him a letter today."

"What did you decide?" Jessa asked. She had nearly forgotten about the Brady-dilemna.

"I decided you were right." Tiff said. "Brady's walk with the Lord is not my responsibility. That's between him and God. If I were to open my heart to him again, knowing he's not a believer, well, that would be risky. It's like Bill said the other day in chapel. I need to guard my heart, and keep it whole and healthy for my future husband. I don't want to give too much of myself to a boyfriend, no matter how much of a sweet-talker he is."

"Good for you." Jessa said. "I think you did the right thing."

"I did tell him I was praying for him, though." Tiff added. "I told him he should join a good youth group."

"Good idea." Jessa said, watching Jay finish prepping the sound equipment up front.

"Thanks." Tiff straightened and tossed her black braid over her shoulder.

"Ouch!" Nate yelped from her other side. "Careful! You whipped me in the eye with that thing!"

"Sorry." Tiff said flatly.

"Hey, wait a minute." Nate said, rubbing his sore eye. "Is that my baseball cap?" He pointed at Hank, who wore a bright-orange hat instead of his usual cowboy hat, and was making his way up to the front. The hat looked bizarre paired with Hank's bushy white-beard and moustache.

"Hey gang." Hank said into the microphone. "I just want to say a few words before we get chapel started. First. Thank you all for being so accommodating with all the schedule changes we had to do around here, when we had to move activities indoors for safety."

"Some of you may have only heard partial versions of what happened. We did have a cougar on site this week, and we lost two of our horses. The danger is passed now, as the cougar has been moved a safe distance away. But it's been a hard week, especially on the barn staff, and I know they really appreciate your support at a time like this." Hank cleared his throat and continued.

"I'd like to take just a moment, if I may, and honour the two horses we lost this week. They may have just been animals; but they were faithful servants to this camp for many years and deserve a fair tribute."

"First, Chester. He was twenty-one years old, and a good reliable horse. Hundreds of campers have ridden him over the years, and he was steady as a rock. Russ, do you have that picture?" Russ was fiddling around at the sound-booth, clicking something into the computer. The projector turned on and a dated picture of Chester appeared, a gleeful camper waving from his back.

"And next, I'd like to honour Dusty." Hank continued, looking at Jessa. "Dusty was twenty-five years old, but you wouldn't know that from the way he acted.

He was strong and fit, and one of the herd-bosses here. That means he was in charge and kept the others in line. He was gentle, sound, and true. Russ, if you can put that picture up."

The screen changed, and Jessa saw a photo of herself, sitting proudly on Dusty's back, a huge smile on her face. It was a picture Hank had taken a month ago when her parents had come to visit. The photo captured Dusty's shaggy brown mane just as a gentle wind ruffled it. Jessa's chest felt tight as the staff gave a collective 'aww' and burst into a supportive applause. Marsha squeezed Jessa's hand tightly, and someone passed her a tissue. Hank continued.

"Thank you Dusty and Chester, for your many years of faithful service to Spruce Ridge Camp. You brought so much joy to so many people. You will be remembered." Hank left the front and Jay stepped up to the microphone.

"Thanks, Hank." Jay said. "And now, let's lift our voices together and worship God." Jessa glanced around, trying to swallow her tears for Dusty. She caught sight of Cory-Lynn and Russ holding hands, and she couldn't help but wonder if their fast-and-furious romance would last. Whether it was truly love, or just a camp-crush.

Thinking back to the whirlwind crush she had had on Wade, she realized she had not been in love. Not really. She hadn't even known him very well. The whole relationship was like a false front; a house of cards that had quickly disintegrated. In her mind, she had convinced herself it was more than just a crush. But in truth, there had been no depth, and now she was left feeling hollow and empty.

Looking back at Jay, Jessa remembered the words he had quoted from the bible; 'Love is patient'. She wondered if he had ever been in love. Since he spoke with such conviction on the subject, she decided he must have some dating experience.

Jessa decided he was right; that the right guy would

pursue her and treasure her heart.

I will guard my heart. Jessa decided. *I will protect it and surrender it to the Lord; so that it is whole for the man I marry one day. And I hope my future husband does the same for me.*

At the end of the service, Jessa saw her mom standing at the back of the dim chapel. She had brought Clark with her, and he was eyeing the girls like a hungry wolf.

"Oh brother!" Jessa rolled her eyes.

"Is that your brother?" Marsha nudged her. "Tiff, check out Jessa's brother."

"No! Don't even go over there." Jessa cried, half-laughing.

"I gotta meet this guy." Tiff said, a mischievous look in her eye, and bounded straight over. Jessa saw Tiff greet her mom, then turn to Clark and say something. She couldn't hear what they were saying, but Clark boldly took Tiff's hand, murmured something, and leant over to kiss it.

"For heaven's sake!" Jessa said to Nate, pointing. "What a player. Tiff's just asking for it. I warned her that he was a heartbreaker!"

"What can ya do?" Nate said. "Sometimes people have to figure things out for themselves. Like I need to figure out how to hide my stuff, apparently." He said sardonically, pointing at the hat Hank was now twirling on his thick finger. "Does he just do that kind of thing to get my goat?"

Hank walked over, almost as if he could hear Nate. "Hey buddy. Lose something?" Hank laughed and tossed the hat into Nate's lap, then turned to Jessa.

"Jessa." Hank said, his expression turning serious.

"Hank." Jessa braced herself for goodbye.

"Jessa, I don't want to try to sway or pressure you." Hank said. "Yet, here we go. I know you've been through a lot. Losing Dusty that way was awful. But Jessa," Hank gathered steam, "I think you should stay. I want you to stay."

"I can't." Jessa whispered. "There's nothing for me here anymore. If I can't ride Dusty, I don't even want to ride anymore. The joy is gone out of it." Jessa's mom had made her way through the crowd and stood beside her.

"You have a gift, Jessa." Hank said firmly. "A natural talent for horsemanship. You're only now beginning to tap into that potential. You have so much more to learn. Don't throw that away."

"I just-"

"And what about Fairlight?" Hank demanded. "I saw you two in that thicket. You called and she answered; she came running to you. You have a special bond with that horse. The kind you'll have with one horse in a lifetime. You really want to walk away from that?"

Jessa's jaw had been clenched, but now she cracked a smile. "You claimed you didn't want to sway or pressure me." Hank stared at her a moment, then threw back his head and guffawed. Jessa thought he looked like Santa, with his white beard and hair.

"I did say that, didn't I?" Hank chuckled. "I guess I lied. I do want to sway you. I want you to stay on for the rest of the summer, and I want you to train Fairlight."

"Train her?" Jessa asked in surprise. "Is she old enough?"

"She's two and a half now. She's ready. You're ready. With the connection you have with her, I know you could do it better than anyone else. I want you to ride her, Jessa."

"I can't believe you think I'm ready for that." Jessa said, astonished and elated. "You would help me?"

"Of course." Hank said. "I know you'll do an amazing job. Come on. Say you'll stay."

Jessa took a deep breath. Her mom remained silent; clearly the decision was hers alone.

Jessa imagined putting Dusty's old saddle on Fairlight, and gentling her. She imagined flying through green fields on Fairlight's back; her rich black mane rippling in the summer breeze. Jessa broke into a jubilant smile.

"Okay Hank, you got me. I'll stay."

The End

DON'T MISS BOOKS ONE AND THREE IN THE SUMMER TRAILS SERIES

Book 1: Summer Trails

Sixteen-year-old Jessa Davies is going to horse camp; and this year she's on staff! She can't wait to spend her summer as a wrangler; riding her favorite horse, goofing off with friends, and basically having a blast. Things go even better than expected when the cutest cowboy at camp starts paying special attention to her!

But things get complicated fast when a co-worker seems to hate her guts. Jessa starts to question everything; from her crush, to whether she even has what it takes to be a wrangler. Tempers run high as manipulation clouds the truth, and Jessa wonders why she ever thought wrangling was good idea. Through it all she is reminded of God´s love as she rides along the summer trails.

Book 3: Trails to Love

Camp is nearly over, and Jessa finds herself the love-target of not one, but several young men. As suitors vie for her attention, Jessa is distracted by something she considers a far-worse crisis; the disastrous new relationship between two people she cares about. As Jessa predicts a catastrophic break-up, old vices resurface and the truth begins to skew. At the same time, a close friend is determined to uncover a guarded secret and pressures Jessa to help. Worst of all, the fear of losing her beloved horse Fairlight looms ever nearer, and Jessa feels powerless to prevent it.

Amidst the struggles of trying to figure out her own heart, a mysterious admirer makes his intentions known, and Jessa is faced with a choice. Can Jessa give her love-life to God, and trust Him to show her which trail to take?

ABOUT THE AUTHOR

Janessa Suderman grew up going to horse camp in the foothills of southern Alberta, Canada, and remembers those years fondly. She bought her first horse Dawn at the age of sixteen, and still gets out riding on her as often as possible. Janessa received her Bachelor of Science in Nursing Degree from Trinity Western University, and works part-time as a nurse. An avid reader from a young age, Janessa kept her younger brother entertained by making up elaborate stories to help him get to sleep. Over the years she has written multiple short stories, poetry, and novels for leisure. The Summer Trails Series is her first published work. She currently lives in southern Alberta with her husband and young son.